Charles Dickens'

A Christmas Carol

Adapted by

John Mortimer

Samuel French — London
New York - Toronto - Hollywood

A CHRISTMAS CAROL

Commissioned and first performed by the Royal Shakespeare Company at the Barbican Theatre, London, on 28th November 1994, financially supported by Unilever, with the following cast:

Ebenezer Scrooge	Clive Francis
Bob Cratchit	Paul Greenwood
Fred, Scrooge's Nephew	Philip Quast
Two Portly Gentlemen	Arthur Cox
	Raymond Mason
The Ghost of Jacob Marley	John Bennett
The Spirit of Christmas Past	Stephen Jenn
Child Scrooge	Steven Geller
	Daniel Whelan
Boy Scrooge	Tom Godfrey
	Ben Reynolds
Young Scrooge	Robert Portal
Headmaster	Raymond Mason
Fan	Vicky Blake
Mr Fezziwig	Raymond Bowers
Dick Wilkins	Peter Warnock
Mrs Fezziwig	Cherry Morris
The Misses Fezziwig	Polly James
	Angela Ridgeon
	Sara Weymouth
Three Young Followers	Michael Geary
	Roger Moss
	Philip Quast
Housemaid	Anita Wright
Baker	John Kane
Cook	Arthur Cox
Milkman	John Warner
Girl	Vicky Blake
Boy	Danny Mertsoy
Belle	Tracy-Ann Oberman
Her Daughter	Sara Weymouth
Her Husband	David Weston

Spirit of Christmas Present	John Kane
Mrs Cratchit	Polly James
Peter	Roger Moss
Martha	Sara Weymouth
Belinda	Vicky Blake
Tiny Tim	Steven Geller
	Daniel Whelan
Little Cratchits	Carla Prosser
	Hannah Everitt
	Patrick Rufey
	Sam Faulkner
Fred's Wife, Scrooge's niece	Sara Weymouth
Miss Rosie, the plump sister	Angela Ridgeon
Mr Topper	Michael Geary
Spirit of Christmas Yet To Come	Peter Warnock
Businessmen	David Weston
	Paul Greenwood
	Raymond Mason
	John Bennett
Jobbins	Raymond Bowers
Staveley	Arthur Cox
Old Joe	John Warner
Charwoman	Cherry Morris
Mrs Dilber	Anita Wright
Undertaker's Man	Stephen Jenn
Boy	Rupert Mealing
Poulterer's Man	Michael Geary
Maid	Vicky Blake
Children	Hannah Gibson
	Oliver Kristian
	David Leslie
	Oliver Palmer
	Charlotte Peters
	Ben Thom

Directed by Ian Judge
Set designed by John Gunter
Costumes designed by Deirdre Clancy
Lighting designed by Nigel Levings
Music composed and arranged by Nigel Hess
Choreography by Lindsay Dolan

CHARACTERS

Ebenezer Scrooge
Bob Cratchit
Fred, Scrooge's nephew
Two Portly Gentlemen
Tiny Tim
Jacob Marley's Ghost
Mrs Cratchit
Peter Cratchit
Belinda Cratchit
Martha Cratchit
Two Smaller Cratchits, a boy and a girl
The Spirit of Christmas Past
Child Scrooge
Ali Baba ⎫
Morgiana ⎪
Robinson Crusoe ⎬ non-speaking
Man Friday ⎪
Sinbad the Sailor ⎭
Young Scrooge
Headmaster
Fan, Scrooge's sister
Fezziwig
Dick Wilkins, Fezziwig's other apprentice
Mrs Fezziwig
Three Misses Fezziwig
Belle, once engaged to Scrooge
Belle's Husband
Belle's Daughter
The Spirit Of Christmas Present
Scrooge's Nephew
Fred's Wife
Miss Rosie, the Plump Sister
Topper
Guests at Fred's Party

Ignorance, a boy
Want, a girl
The Spirit Of Christmas Yet to Come
First Businessman
Second Businessman
Third Businessman
Fourth Businessman
First Important Man
Second Important Man
Man on Scrooge's Corner of the Exchange
Old Joe, a receiver of stolen property
Charwoman
Mrs Dilber, a laundress
An Undertaker's Man
Caroline
William
Their Child
Boy in Sunday Clothes
Poulterer's Man
Fred's Maid
Sailors, Miners, Lighthouse Men, etc.

The play is set in London and in and around a country town. The visits to a miner's cottage, a lighthouse and a ship at sea are done without scenery.

The main action takes place in 1843. But Scrooge is a child in the 1770s and a young man in the 1790s.

PRODUCTION NOTES

At the Barbican, the play was presented with elaborate stage machinery, houses and scenery that rose into the air and a revolve. The play can be presented far more simply, on a bare stage with furniture brought on and off when it is needed, for the office, Scrooge's bedroom, etc. The following text indicates when the scenes are played, but how they are set will depend on the intention and resources of each production.

The Chorus
The Chorus consists of the actors who are not playing named parts at the time—so all the cast play a part (or parts) and also take part in the Chorus. The allotment of the Chorus lines can be filled in in the empty brackets according to the number of actors and the Director's decision. Only one actor speaks at a time.

Music
In order to give as complete a record as possible of the Royal Shakespeare Company's production of *A Christmas Carol*, the composer, Nigel Hess, has kindly supplied full details of all the *vocal* music used in the first production. In all, some seventy-five minutes of original music was played.

It is not obligatory to use any, or all, of this music in productions of the play. Other carols and music of the period can be substituted. However, a note of where Nigel Hess's music may be obtained is given on page ix. **Please read the notices regarding the use of copyright music on pages ix and x carefully.**

Vocal Music used in the original production of *A Christmas Carol*

Act I

1. God Rest You Merry,Gentlemen	Music/lyrics: traditional
2. Alas We Bless	Music: Nigel Hess
	Lyrics: adapted from *The Wassail* by
	Robert Herrick (1591-1674)
3. Veni Veni	Music/lyrics: traditional (to the tune of
	O Come, O Come Emmanuel)
4. Angels From The Realms of	Music: traditional/Nigel Hess
Glory/O Oriens Solare	Lyrics: traditional
5. And Here is to Dobbin	Music: Nigel Hess
	Lyrics: traditional (from *The Glouces-*
	tershire Wassail)
6. There Was An Old Man	Music:Nigel Hess
	Lyrics: traditional (adapted from *The*
	Somerset Wassail)
7. Beloved Eye, Beloved Star	Music: Nigel Hess
	Lyrics: J Oxenford (from the song
	Thou Art So Near and Yet So Far)
8. God Bless the Master	Music: Nigel Hess
	Lyrics:traditional (from *This New*
	Christmas Carol)
9. Angels From the Realms of	Music: traditional/Mendelssohn/
Glory/Hark The Herald	Nigel Hess
Angels Sing	Lyrics: traditional/Charles Wesley

Act II

1. Silent Night	Music: Franz Xaver Gruber (1787-
	1863)
	Lyrics: Joseph Mohr (1792-1849)
2. All Hail to the Days	Music: Nigel Hess
	Lyrics: Tom Durfey (1653-1723) and
	others (from *The Praise of Christmas*)
3. Past Three O'Clock	Music/lyrics traditional

4. If Bethlehem Were Here Today	Music: Nigel Hess
	Lyrics: Elizabeth Madox Roberts
	(freely adapted from *Christmas Morning*) 1922
5. While Shepherds Watched	Music: Christopher Tye (c 1500-1573)
	Lyrics: Nahum Tate (?) 1652-1715
6. O Master and Missus	Music: Nigel Hess
	Lyrics: traditional (from *The Somerset Wassail*)
7. I Saw Three Ships	Music/lyrics: traditional
8. Our Wassail Cup	Music: Nigel Hess
	Lyrics: traditional (from *Wassail Song*)
9. Puer Nobis Nascitur	Music/lyrics: traditional (to the tune of *Unto Us is Born a Son*)
10. Beloved Eye, Beloved Star	as above
11. Love and Joy	Music: Nigel Hess
	Lyrics: traditional (from *Wassail Song*)
12. God Bless The Master	as above

All the newly composed music for *A Christmas Carol* is published by Myra Music Ltd, administered by Bucks Music Ltd.

Applications to use this newly composed music in productions of *A Christmas Carol* must be made to Bucks Music at the above address. A licence issued by Samuel French Ltd to perform the play does NOT include permission to use any copyright music within the production.

Other plays by John Mortimer published by
Samuel French Ltd:

The Bells of Hell
Cat Among the Pigeons (*translator*)
Collaborators
Come As You Are
The Dock Brief
Edwin
The Fear of Heaven
A Flea in Her Ear (*translator*)
I Spy
Knightsbridge
A Little Hotel on the Side (*translator*)
Lunch Hour
One To Another (*sketches; co-author*)
Two Stars For Comfort
A Voyage Round My Father
What Shall We Tell Caroline?

ACT I

London

There is a coffin on the empty stage. It is Marley's funeral and Scrooge is the chief mourner. The Chorus are on stage and circle round him as they speak

( ) **Chorus** Marley was dead, to begin with.
( ) **Chorus** There is no doubt whatever about that.
( ) **Chorus** The register of his burial was signed by the clergyman——
( ) **Chorus** —the clerk——
( ) **Chorus** —the undertaker——
( ) **Chorus** —and the Chief Mourner.
( ) **Chorus** Ebenezer Scrooge signed it.
( ) **Chorus** And his name's good up at the Exchange for anything he puts his hand to.
( ) **Chorus** Old Marley was as dead as a doornail.
( ) **Chorus** Mind! I don't mean to say, of my own knowledge, what there is particularly dead about a doornail.
( ) **Chorus** I might have been inclined, for myself, to regard a *coffin* nail as the deadest piece of ironmongery in the trade.
( ) **Chorus** No doubt the wisdom of our ancestors is in the simile; and my unhallowed hands shall not disturb it, or the country's done for.
( ) **Chorus** There is no doubt that Marley was dead.
( ) **Chorus** This must be distinctly understood or nothing wonderful can come of the story we are going to relate.
( ) **Chorus** So I repeat emphatically, Jacob Marley was dead as a doornail.

Scrooge sprinkles earth on the coffin

( ) **Chorus** Scrooge knew he was dead?

( ) **Chorus** Of course he did. How could it be otherwise?

( ) **Chorus** Scrooge and he were partners for I don't know how many years.

( ) **Chorus** Scrooge was his sole executor, his sole administrator, his sole assign, his sole residuary legatee, his sole friend——

( ) **Chorus** —and his sole mourner...

Scrooge turns away from the graveside. He moves down stage, meets a prosperous looking man from the Chorus, and engages him in conversation

( ) **Chorus** And even Scrooge was not so dreadfully cut up by the sad event!

Scrooge and the prosperous man shake hands

( ) **Chorus** He was an excellent man of business on the very day of the funeral, and solemnized it with an undoubted bargain!

The prosperous man pays money to Scrooge, which Scrooge counts carefully

( ) **Chorus** Oh, he's a tight-fisted hand at the grindstone is Scrooge.

( ) **Chorus** Hard and sharp as flint——

( ) **Chorus** —for which no steel ever struck out a generous fire.

( ) **Chorus** Secret and self-contained——

( ) **Chorus** —and solitary as an oyster.

( ) **Chorus** The cold within him freezes his old features, stiffens his gait, makes his eyes red, his thin lips blue——

( ) **Chorus** —and speaks out clearly in his grating voice.

( ) **Chorus** He carries his low temperature always about with him.

( ) **Chorus** He ices his office in the dog days and doesn't thaw it out one degree at Christmas.

Scrooge moves down stage towards the entrance of his warehouse, through the Chorus, who are dispersed on the stage. He passes through them ungreeted and unnoticed

( ) **Chorus** No one ever stops him in the street to say——

( ) **Chorus** My dear Scrooge. How are you?

( ) **Chorus** When will you come to see me?
( ) **Chorus (Beggar)** No beggars implore him to bestow a trifle.
( ) **Chorus (Child)** No children ask him what o'clock it is.
( ) **Chorus (Blind man)** Even the blind man's dog appears to know him——
( ) **Chorus** —and pulls its owner away as though to say——
( ) **Chorus** —"No eye at all is better than the evil eye of Scrooge."
( ) **Chorus** He passes behind our backs like a cold shiver.
( ) **Chorus** To edge his way along the crowded paths of life, warning all human sympathy to keep its distance.
( ) **Chorus** That, ladies and gentlemen, is "nuts" to Scrooge.

Scrooge arrives at his warehouse door. We see the sign over it: "Scrooge and Marley"

( ) **Chorus** Scrooge and Marley.
( ) **Chorus** Scrooge won't have Marley's name painted out.
( ) **Chorus** Why go to the expense?
( ) **Chorus** Some may call him "Scrooge" and some "Marley".
( ) **Chorus** It makes no difference. Provided their credit's good and they can pay on the nail!
( ) **Chorus** Or the coffin nail, perhaps.

SCENE 2

Scrooge's office

Fog rises outside. A clock chimes three

The Chorus stamps to keep warm. Scrooge sits at his desk and starts to do his accounts in a huge ledger

( ) **Chorus** Once upon a time—of all the good days of the year, on Christmas Eve—Scrooge sits busy in his counting house...
( ) **Chorus** Jacob Marley has been dead a good seven year.
( ) **Chorus** It's cold, bleak, biting weather: foggy withal.
( ) **Chorus** Scrooge can hear the people in the court outside go wheezing up and down.
( ) **Chorus** Beating their hands upon their breasts——

( ) **Chorus** —and stamping their feet upon the paving stones to warm them.
( ) **Chorus** The City clocks have just gone three, but it's dark already: it hasn't been light all day.
( ) **Chorus** The fog comes pouring in at every chink and keyhole.

Scrooge unlocks a large tin box, and starts to count the money in it

( ) **Chorus** External heat and cold have little influence on Scrooge.
( ) **Chorus** Foul weather doesn't know where to take advantage over him.

Lights up on Bob Cratchit's small office where a candle is burning

Bob Cratchit is working at his table

( ) **Chorus** The door of Scrooge's counting house is open so he may keep his eye upon his clerk, who in a dismal little cell beyond...
( ) **Chorus** A sort of tank——
( ) **Chorus** Is copying letters.
( ) **Chorus** Scrooge has a very small fire——
( ) **Chorus** —but the clerk's fire is so very much smaller that it looks like one coal...

Bob Cratchit blows on his fingers, shivers, then plucks up courage and picks up a small shovel from his grate. He knocks on Scrooge's open door, fearfully, and then coughs to attract Scrooge's attention

Scrooge What is it, Cratchit?
Cratchit Could you see your way clear, Mr Scrooge? In your great generosity, sir? To spare me a few coals for my fireplace, which is now empty, sir?
Scrooge No, I could not see my way clear! And if you take time off your work, Cratchit, to come in here with exorbitant demands—then you and I must part company. Is that what you want?
Cratchit Not at all, Mr Scrooge. By no means. Thank you for your time, sir. (*He goes dolefully back to his office*)

Scrooge is working. Cratchit puts on his long white scarf and tries to warm his hands by his candle

( ) **Chorus** The clerk put on his white comforter, and tried to warm himself at the candle.

( ) **Chorus** In which office, not being a man of strong imagination, he failed.

Scrooge's Nephew enters Scrooge's office

Nephew A Merry Christmas, Uncle! God save you!

Scrooge (*not looking up from his work*) Bah! Humbug!

The Nephew blows out his cheeks

( ) **Chorus** He has so heated himself with walking through the fog and frost, this nephew of Scrooge's, that he's all in a glow.

Nephew Christmas "humbug", Uncle? You don't mean that, surely?

Scrooge I do. "Merry Christmas"? What reason have you to be merry? You're poor enough!

Nephew Come then. What right do you have to be dismal? You're rich enough!

Scrooge (*glaring at him*) Bah! (*He returns to work*) Humbug!

Nephew Don't be cross, Uncle!

Scrooge What else can I be? (*He throws down his pen*) When I live in a world of fools? Merry Christmas! Out upon Merry Christmas! What's Christmas to you but a time for paying bills without money? A time for finding yourself a year older and not an hour richer? A time for balancing your books and having every item in 'em proved dead against you? I wish every idiot who goes about with "Merry Christmas" on his lips should be boiled with his own pudding, and buried with a stake of holly through his heart. So he should!

Nephew Uncle...

Scrooge Nephew! (*He picks up his pen again*) You keep "Merry Christmas" in your own way and I'll keep it in mine.

Nephew You keep it? But, Uncle, you don't keep it!

Scrooge Let me leave it out, then. Much good it has ever done you.

Nephew There are many things I haven't profited by, I'm sure, Uncle. But I believe Christmas is a *good* time. A kind, forgiving, pleasant, charitable time. The only time I know of when we all seem by one consent to open our hearts freely—and think of people poorer than us as fellow passengers to the grave. Not a strange race of creatures bound on other journeys which don't concern us at all! So, Uncle. Christmas may never have put a scrap of gold or silver in my pocket. But I believe it *has* done me good. And *will* do me good. So I say, God bless it!

Bob Cratchit applauds so loudly that he succeeds in blowing out his guttering candle. Scrooge goes to the door of the clerk's room and pokes his head in, furious

Scrooge Let me hear one more sound from you and I'll give you a surprise Christmas present. Instant dismissal! Without a reference! (*He bangs the door shut and goes back to his Nephew*) You're quite a powerful speaker, sir. I wonder you don't go into Parliament.

Cratchit tries to relight the candle in his room

Nephew Don't be angry, Uncle. Dine with us tomorrow.
Scrooge Don't insult my intelligence! (*He sits at his desk*) What? Waste a day singing silly songs and stuffing down pudding and playing hunt the slipper with a pack of spoiled little brats! Seeing you in hell would be a pleasant alternative.

Cratchit has managed to relight the candle

Nephew But why... *Why?*
Scrooge Why did you get married, Nephew?
Nephew Because I fell in love, Uncle!
Scrooge (*sarcastically*) Because you fell in love? Good afternoon!
Nephew Nay, Uncle you never came to see me *before* that happened. Why give it as a reason for not coming now.
Scrooge Good afternoon!
Nephew I want nothing from you. I ask nothing of you. Why cannot we be friends...?
Scrooge Good afternoon!
Nephew I am sorry with all my heart to find you so resolute. We have never had any quarrel to which I have been a party. But I have made the trial in homage to Christmas, and I'll keep my Christmas humour to the last. So a Merry Christmas, Uncle!
Scrooge Good afternoon!
Nephew And a Happy New Year!

Scrooge Cratchit! Will you wake up and let this relative out of my sight.

Cratchit comes into Scrooge's office

Nephew A Merry Christmas, Mr Cratchit!
Cratchit Merry Christmas, sir.
Scrooge There's my clerk! Fifteen shillings a week with a wife and brats ... talking about "A Merry Christmas"? Now I think I'll retire to Bedlam in search of some sanity.

The Nephew exits. As he goes, he passes the two Portly Gentlemen on their way to Scrooge's office

( ) **Chorus** The lunatic, in letting Scrooge's nephew out, lets the two other people in.

The Portly Gentlemen move into Scrooge's office

Cratchit goes back to his "tank", looking at them curiously

First Portly Gent Two portly gentlemen, pleasant to behold——
Second Portly Gent —now stand with their hats off in Scrooge's office.
Scrooge Good afternoon!
First Portly Gent Merry Christmas!
Second Portly Gent Merry Christmas.

They stand, holding their hats

Scrooge (*muttering*) Bedlamites!
First Portly Gent Scrooge and Marley. We believe...
Second Portly Gent Have we the pleasure of addressing Mr Scrooge or Mr Marley?
Scrooge Mr Marley has been dead these seven years. He died seven years ago this very night.
First Portly Gent And we have no doubt his liberality is well represented by his surviving partner. (*He hands a paper to Scrooge*)
( ) **Chorus** At the ominous word "liberality", Scrooge frowned, shook his head, and gave the Portly Gentleman back his credentials.
Second Portly Gent We are representatives of the Society for the Relief of Poverty.

Scrooge Are you indeed? (*He goes back to work*)

Second Portly Gent The Ragged Children's Clothing Charity.

First Portly Gent The Relief of Starvation in City Streets.

Second Portly Gent The Gentlewomen's Provision of Simple Fare to the Deserving Poor.

Scrooge (*not looking up from his work*) Humbug!

First Portly Gent At this festive season of the year, Mr Scrooge. It is Scrooge, is it not?

Scrooge Yes, it's Scrooge.

Second Portly Gent Mr Marley is deceased. Yes, of course, you said so.

First Portly Gent Unfortunately deceased.

Second Portly Gent At this season of the year. It is more than usually desirable that we should make some slight provision for the poor and homeless.

First Portly Gent Who suffer greatly at the present time.

Second Portly Gent Many are in want of common necessities, sir.

First Portly Gent Hundreds are in want of common comforts, sir.

Scrooge Poor people?

First Portly Gent Yes, Mr Scrooge.

Scrooge Beggars?

Second Portly Gent Alas, yes, Mr Scrooge.

Scrooge Are there no prisons?

First Portly Gent Plenty of prisons, sir.

Scrooge And the workhouses. Are they still in operation?

Second Portly Gent They are still, sir.

First Portly Gent We wish we could say they were not.

Scrooge And the Poor Law. In full vigour, is it? And the Treadmill. Still turning nicely, I hope.

Second Portly Gent Both very busy, sir.

Scrooge Oh, I'm very glad to hear it. I was afraid from what you said something had gone wrong with those admirable institutions.

First Portly Gent But they scarcely furnish Christmas cheer to the multitude.

Second Portly Gent At this time of the year, Want is keenly felt and Abundance rejoices.

Scrooge sweeps his money into the drawer of his desk

First Portly Gent What shall we put you down for?

Scrooge slams the drawer shut and locks it

Scrooge Nothing!

First Portly Gent (*smiling*) We understand.

Second Portly Gent (*smiling*) An anonymous gift? That's very generous!

First Portly Gent A modest benefactor, Mr Scrooge! Who would do good by stealth.

Second Portly Gent And doesn't wish to see his name published.

Scrooge (*in an outburst*) I wish to be left alone! I don't make merry at Christmas. And I can't afford to make idle people merry. I support the Poor House, sir. And the Treadmill. And the Gaols. They cost enough, in all conscience. Let those who are badly off make use of such luxuries!

Second Portly Gent Many would rather die, sir. Than go to the Poor House.

Scrooge If that's what they'd prefer... By all means let them do it! Why not? Decrease the surplus population. It's not my business if they'd rather die. It's enough for a man to understand his own business and mine occupies me continually. Good afternoon, gentlemen.

First Portly Gent Merry——

Scrooge Good afternoon!

Second Portly Gent Seeing clearly that it would be useless to pursue their quest...

First Portly Gent The Portly Gentlemen withdrew...

They exit

Scrooge goes back to his desk. He rules lines on paper to set out his accounts. The street is empty, bleaker, with a little sifting of snow

( ) **Chorus** Foggier yet, and colder.

( ) **Chorus** Piercing, searching, biting cold.

A Boy moves towards Scrooge's door, singing "God Rest You Merry, Gentlemen"

( ) **Chorus** The owner of one scant young nose...

( ) **Chorus** Gnawed and mumbled by the hungry cold...

( ) **Chorus** As bones are gnawed by dogs...

( ) **Chorus** Stooped down at Scrooge's keyhole...
( ) **Chorus** To regale him with a carol.

Scrooge seizes a big ruler off his desk, rushes to the door, flings it open, and raises the ruler to threaten the boy

Scrooge Humbug!

The boy retreats

Scrooge goes back to work. The clock strikes six

( ) **Chorus** At length the hour of shutting up the counting house arrived.
( ) **Chorus** With an ill will, Scrooge dismounted from his stool.

Scrooge does so

( ) **Chorus** And tacitly admitted the fact to the expectant clerk.

Scrooge goes to Cratchit's door and makes a reluctant gesture of dismissal. Cratchit immediately puts on his hat and snuffs out the candle

Scrooge You'll want a day off tomorrow, I don't doubt...?
Cratchit If it's quite convenient, sir.
Scrooge It's not quite convenient! More than that. It's not fair. If I was to stop you half a crown for it, you'd start squealing, I'll be bound. You'd think yourself ill used. Well, sir. Don't you think I'm ill used? Having to pay you for lying idle?
Cratchit (*smiling faintly*) Christmas is but once a year, sir.
Scrooge (*putting on his hat and coat*) So you can pick a man's pocket every twenty-fifth of December? A poor excuse. And I suppose you're asking for the whole day. What? Be two hours earlier next morning. When sanity returns to the world. That's all I've got to say to you!
Cratchit Happy——
Scrooge (*going*) Bah!

Scrooge exits

Singers   Now to the Lord sing praises,
                               All you within this place,

And with true love and brotherhood
Each other now embrace.
The holy tide of Christmas
All others doth efface.
O tidings of comfort and joy, comfort and joy,
O tidings of comfort and joy.

SCENE 3

The street. Scrooge is leaving his office

Cratchit starts to lock up. Scrooge makes his way through the crowds in the street. As he passes, groups are singing snatches of "God Rest You Merry, Gentlemen", much to Scrooge's fury

( ) **Chorus** Meanwhile the fog and darkness thicken so, that people run about with flaring links.

( ) **Chorus** Proffering their services to go before the horses in the carriages and conduct them on their way.

( ) **Chorus** The ancient tower of a church...

( ) **Chorus** Whose gruff old bell was always peeping slyly down at Scrooge out of a Gothic window in the wall...

( ) **Chorus** Strikes the hours and quarters in the clouds with tremulous vibrations afterwards...

( ) **Chorus** As if its teeth are chattering in its frozen head up there.

( ) **Chorus** The cold becomes intense.

During the following Chorus lines, Cratchit comes away from the warehouse, warms his hands at the brazier and then joins a group of boys sliding on the ice. Scrooge arrives at his chophouse. The waiter takes his order, and brings Scrooge his chop and a newspaper

( ) **Chorus** The brightness of the shops, where holly sprigs and berries crackled in the lamp heat of the windows...

( ) **Chorus** Make pale faces ruddy as they pass.

( ) **Chorus** The Lord Mayor...

( ) **Chorus** In the stronghold of the mighty Mansion House...

( ) **Chorus** Gives orders to his fifty cooks and butlers...

( ) **Chorus** To keep Christmas as a Lord Mayor's household should.

Scrooge throws down his newspaper and starts reading his bank book

( ) **Chorus** Scrooge has read his newspaper, and beguiles the evening with his favourite reading.
( ) **Chorus** His bank statement!

Tiny Tim appears

We see Cratchit sliding on the ice. Tiny Tim watches him

( ) **Chorus** Cratchit, with the long ends of his comforter dangling below his waist...
( ) **Chorus** For he boasts no greatcoat...
( ) **Chorus** Goes down the ice slide in Cornhill, twenty times...
( ) **Chorus** Between a lane of boys.
( ) **Chorus** In honour of it's being Christmas Eve.

Tiny Tim, leaning on his crutch, watches his father and claps. Scrooge finishes his dinner

Scrooge Waiter. Toothpick!

The waiter appears with a toothpick

Cratchit stops sliding, picks up Tiny Tim, and carries him off

Scrooge pays the waiter, failing to give him a tip

Scrooge exits

The waiter makes rude gestures at Scrooge's retreating back

Music: "Alas We Bless"

SCENE 4

Scrooge is walking home, picking his teeth

Three or four children, who have been watching the sliding and taking part, follow him, imitating his walk and his tooth picking, jumping and running behind him

Singers   Alas! we bless, but see none here
                               That brings us either ale or beer;
                               Let's leave a longer time to wait,
                               While rust and cobwebs bind the gate.

( ) **Chorus** Scrooge is going home to bed.

( ) **Chorus** He lives in the dusty rooms, that were the home of his dead partner!

( ) **Chorus** In a gloomy pile of a building, up a yard where it had no business to be...

( ) **Chorus (Child)** You can't help fancying that it ran there when it was a young house, playing hide and seek with other houses and forgot the way out.

Singers   Where chimneys do forever weep
                               For want of warmth, and no eyes sleep.
                               It is in vain to sing or stay
                               Our cold feet here; but we'll away.

( ) **Chorus** The yard is so dark that even Scrooge, who knows its every stone, has to grope with his hands.

Singers   The time will come when you'll be sad
                               And reckon this for fortune bad,
                               To have lost the good ye might have had.

( ) **Chorus** By the way—the door knocker.

( ) **Chorus** It's a fact there's nothing particular about the door knocker. Except it's very large!

( ) **Chorus** Scrooge has seen it every night and morning.

( ) **Chorus** And Scrooge has as little of what's called fancy about him as any man in the City of London.

( ) **Chorus** Including the Corporation.

( ) **Chorus** So let anyone explain why Scrooge can see...

During the following passage, Scrooge puts his key in the lock

( ) **Chorus** Having his key in the lock...
( ) **Chorus** Should see...
( ) **Chorus** Not a knocker, but...

The knocker changes, and becomes Marley's face. It's a livid greyish colour, its grey hair is ruffled, its spectacles pushed up on his forehead. It is staring at Scrooge with grey, expressionless eyes

Marley Marley's face!

Scrooge stands staring at it. The children retreat further into the shadows during the following

( ) **Chorus** With a dismal light about it...
( ) **Chorus** Glowing like a bad lobster in the dark!
( ) **Chorus** Though the eyes are open, they don't move.
( ) **Chorus** That and its livid colour, makes it horrible...
All Horrible...
Scrooge Jacob Marley! Is that you, Jacob? What're you playing at, my old partner? Don't come bothering me now. You're dead as a coffin nail, remember.

Marley's face fades. One of the children comes into the light

( ) **Chorus** It's a knocker again.
Scrooge That's better, Jacob, you old devil. Never there at all, was you? (*He opens the door and looks carefully at the inside of it. Then he lights a candle and examines the back of the door more closely*) If you had've been there, I'd've expected to see your cursed pigtail sticking out behind you. (*He moves the candle to see more clearly*) No pigtail! And therefore no Jacob. *Quod Erat Demonstrandum.* So far as all ghosts and night-walkers go ... it's humbug! Pooh! Pooh! (*He slams the door shut*)

The sound of the door and the hugely amplified sounds of his "Pooh! Pooh!" echo and re-echo. Scrooge, his candle in his hand, starts to go up the dark stairs towards his bedroom

( ) **Chorus** Some talk of driving a coach and horses up a good old flight of stairs.

( ) **Chorus** But I mean to say you could get a hearse up that staircase.

Scrooge stops. He sees the shape of a hearse on a wall

( ) **Chorus** Is that why Scrooge thinks he can see a hearse in the gloom?
Scrooge Humbug... (*He moves on up the stairs*)
( ) **Chorus** Of course, it's dark.
( ) **Chorus** Scrooge likes it dark.
( ) **Chorus** Darkness comes cheap.

Scrooge moves up to his bedroom

Scene 5

Scrooge's bedroom and sitting-room

During the following Chorus passage, Scrooge searches his rooms, getting into his night clothes, finally settling down with his gruel by the fire in his sitting-room

Scrooge Sitting-room, all as it should be. Nobody under the table! Nobody under the sofa!
( ) **Chorus** A small fire in the grate.
( ) **Chorus** Spoon and basin ready for the little saucepan of gruel up on the hob.
( ) **Chorus** Scrooge has a cold in his head.
( ) **Chorus** Nobody under the bed!
( ) **Chorus** Nobody in the closet!
( ) **Chorus** Nobody in his dressing gown, which is hanging in a suspicious attitude against the wall!
( ) **Chorus** Quite satisfied, Scrooge sits down before the fire to take his gruel.

Scrooge is by the fire in the sitting-room

( ) **Chorus** It's a very low fire, nothing on such a bitter night.
( ) **Chorus** He is obliged to sit over it, and brood over it, before he can extract the least sensation of warmth from such a handful of fuel.

*Scrooge paces the room. He sits again. He throws back his head, and
starts at a bell*

( ) **Chorus** His glance happens to rest upon a bell.
( ) **Chorus** A disused bell, that hangs in his room.
( ) **Chorus** And communicates, for some purpose now forgotten, with
a chamber in the highest storey of the house.
( ) **Chorus** It is with great astonishment…
( ) **Chorus** And inexplicable dread…
( ) **Chorus** That Scrooge sees the bell begin to swing.
( ) **Chorus** It swings so softly it hardly makes a sound.
( ) **Chorus** But now it rings out loudly!
( ) **Chorus** And so does every bell in the house!
( ) **Chorus** Who's ringing the bells…?
Scrooge It's humbug still! I won't believe it.

*The bells stop ringing. There's the sound of a door slamming, somewhere
in the bowels of the house*

( ) **Chorus** Who slams the door?

Sound of chains being dragged across the floor

( ) **Chorus** And drags chains when there's no prison hereabouts?

*Marley's Ghost appears in the shadows at the bottom of the stairs. His
jaw is held up by a bandage tied on top of his head. He wears a jacket
and waistcoat, tights, and boots with their tassels bristling. His pigtail
sticks out behind him. His body seems to be hollow, so you can see a
white, glowing backbone where his stomach ought to be. He has a chain
round his waist so long that it's a tail of keys, padlocks, ledgers, deeds
and heavy purses. We hear his footsteps as he goes up the stairs*

( ) **Chorus** Footsteps…
( ) **Chorus** Scrooge never held with stair carpet…
( ) **Chorus** So he can hear the footsteps on the stairs.

*Scrooge is sitting by his feeble bedroom fire as the Ghost comes up the
stairs and through the locked door behind Scrooge, who doesn't look
round. When he speaks, it is cold and caustic*

Scrooge What do you want with me?
Marley Much.
Scrooge Who are you?
Marley Rather ask me who I *was*.
Scrooge All right then. Who *were* you?
Marley In life I was your partner. Jacob Marley.

Scrooge turns and looks at the Ghost for the first time

Scrooge Jacob Marley! I always knew you had no bowels. Now I see it
   clearly.
Marley You don't believe in me?
Scrooge I don't!
Marley Why do you doubt your senses?
Scrooge Because little things upset them. How do I know you're not a
   mere—indigestion? A hard gristle of chop, a blot of mustard, a crumb
   of cheese, a fragment of underdone potato? You're no more than a
   stomach upset. More gravy than graveyard, you! You see this tooth-
   pick?
Marley I do.
Scrooge You're not looking at it.
Marley I see it all the same.
Scrooge Well. I have but to swallow this to be persecuted for the rest of
   my days, persecuted by legions of restless spirits and hobgoblins!
   Stomach upset. What do you say about that?

*The Ghost gives a terrible cry of anguish and rattles his chain—so
amplified that Scrooge holds on to his chair. Then the Ghost undoes the
bandage so its jaw drops on to its chest with a great clang. Scrooge is now
on his knees*

   Dreadful apparition! Why do you trouble me?
Marley Man of worldly mind! Do you believe in me or not?
Scrooge I suppose I do. Got no choice, have I? But Jacob. Couldn't you
   have stayed at home? I mean—what's the reason for this visit? It's
   getting late and I've been hard at work.

Unearthly music during Marley's speech

Marley To warn you, Ebenezer Scrooge! Learn from me. My spirit never walked beyond our counting house. It never roved beyond our money-changing hole. So I'm condemned to wander through the world. To see what I might have shared on earth and turned to happiness.

Scrooge But Jacob! You was always a good businessman.

The music stops

Marley It was not enough. I should have known. Mankind was my true business. Charity, Mercy, Benevolence. These were all my business. Money making was but a drop in the wide ocean of my proper business.

Scrooge I beg you, Jacob. Don't be flowery with me. Why are you in chains?

Marley I wear the chain I made in my life. I made it. Link by link. Yard by yard. I made it of my own free will, every day I made money and forgot the poor.

Scrooge And you has to travel every day. Wearing that?

Marley Would you know the weight and length of the stong coil you will bear yourself. It was heavy and as long as this seven Christmas Eves ago. You have laboured on it since. It is a ponderous chain.

Scrooge Don't be hard on me! Speak comfort to me, Jacob.

Marley I have none to give. I cannot linger anywhere. I have very little more time to deal with you.

Scrooge Don't be hard on me. I beg you. And not too flowery, mind.

Marley At this time of the rolling year, why did I walk through crowds of fellow beings with my eyes turned down and never raise them to that blessed star which took the Wise Men to a home of poverty...?

Scrooge (*protesting mildly*) That's flowery... Jacob. Very flowery!

Marley I'm here to warn you. To give you a chance of escaping my fate. And to bring you some hope.

Scrooge You were always a good friend to me. Thankee, Jacob. A bit of hope would come very welcome! Thankee...

Marley You will be haunted by three spirits.

Scrooge Oh. Yes? What? Is *that* the hope you spoke of?

Marley It is!

Scrooge Then thankee very much. I'd rather do without it.

Marley Expect the first tomorrow. When the bell tolls one.

Scrooge Couldn't I take all three at once, Jacob? And get 'em over and done with. Like nasty medicine...

Marley Expect the second the next night at the same hour. And the third the night following. W_{..}en the last stroke of midnight no longer echoes. Look to see me no more, Ebenezer Scrooge. But for your own sake. Remember me. Remember me. Remember me.

Scrooge, still on his knees, looks up. He sees Marley tie the bandage again and his teeth snap together loudly. Then Marley gathers up his chain, winds it round his arm and beckons Scrooge to follow him as he walks backwards towards the window, which opens of its own accord. There is a sound of wailing and lamentation

Scene 6

( ) **Chorus** The air is filled with phantoms wandering hither and thither in restless haste.

( ) **Chorus** And moaning as they go.

( ) **Chorus** Every one of them wears chains like Marley's Ghost.

( ) **Chorus** Some of them are linked together.

( ) **Chorus** They might be guilty government ministers.

( ) **Chorus** None are free.

( ) **Chorus** Scrooge has known many of them during their lives.

A young mother sits on Scrooge's doorstep, hugging a small baby and trying to keep it warm

( ) **Chorus** Scrooge has been quite familiar with one old ghost in a white waistcoat.

( ) **Chorus** With a monstrous safe attached to its ankle.

The Ghost, weighed down with the safe, sinks to the woman and holds out its arms to her

Marley Marley who flies down to help a wretched woman with an infant whom it saw below.

The Ghost is snatched up again

( ) **Chorus** And cries piteously when it's snatched away.

( ) **Chorus** The misery for them all is...

( ) **Chorus** That they seek to interfere for good, in human matters.
( ) **Chorus** And have lost the power forever.

Marley's Ghost rises, floats out of the window and joins the other phantoms

The Ghost vanishes. The sky is empty

Scrooge bangs the window shut. He bolts it. He examines the door the Ghost came through. It's bolted and locked

Scrooge Humb——

He cannot finish the word. He jumps into bed, without undressing, and pulls the curtains shut and so disappears from our sight

Sound of the church clock chiming a quarter

Music: "Veni, Veni"

SCENE 7

Scrooge's bedroom

The bed curtains part and Scrooge peers out, nervously now. He is wearing a nightcap and his night-shirt.

The clock chimes a second quarter

Scrooge Ding dong. Half past o' what I wonder? I took a long sleep. Didn't I? (*He rubs his eyes*) When I got there...

The clock chimes three-quarters

Ding dong. Quarter to it. (*He looks towards the window*) Must be morning. Dark as hell at Christmas.

The clock chimes the hour

Ding dong. The hour itself! And nothing else.

The clock booms once—deep, hollow, melancholy

One o'clock? Can't be possible! It was near two when I went to bed with all the disturbance... Can I have slept some twenty-three hours, can I? Where's my watch? Old Marley's watch once... But he no longer has a use for it. (*He pulls the curtain back further and finds a watch under his pillow. He shakes it, then puts it to his ear*) Watch says one also. The clocks run mad like people over Christmas... Agh!

The side curtains of his bed are drawn back

( ) **Chorus** The curtains of his bed were drawn aside, I tell you, by a hand!
( ) **Chorus** Not the curtains at his feet, nor the curtains at his back...
( ) **Chorus** But those to which his face was addressed.
( ) **Chorus** The curtains of his bed were drawn aside...

A strange Light from an extraordinary figure floods the scene—the Spirit of Christmas Past

It looks like an old man shrunk to the size of a child. White hair hangs down its back, but its face has no wrinkles. Its arms, legs, and feet are bare. It wears a white tunic, trimmed with spring flowers and a belt which shines beautifully. It carries a branch of green holly. The light which has illuminated Scrooge's bedroom comes from the top of its head. Under one arm it carries something like a giant dunce's cap, and a large candle snuffer

( ) **Chorus** And Scrooge, starting up into a half recumbent attitude...
( ) **Chorus** Found himself face to face with the unearthly visitor who drew them...
( ) **Chorus** As close to it as I am now to you...
( ) **Chorus** And I am standing in the spirit at your elbow.
Scrooge You! Are you the visitor I was told to expect?
Spirit (*in a gentle, but somehow distant voice*) I am.
Scrooge Who are *you* then?
Spirit I am the Ghost of Christmas Past.

Scrooge Long past?
Spirit No. Your past. (*It moves into the room*)

Scrooge moves after it, leaving the bed. Still fearful, he tries to be polite

Scrooge Please Spirit. No need to stand there so respectful. Be covered,
Spirit. Please put your cap on your head.
Spirit My cap? You want to put out my light so quickly? You—one of
those dim spirits who tried to make a cap to cover my flame and make
the whole world dreary...? You, the great fire extinguisher? Don't ask
me that.
Scrooge Please! Don't trouble yourself any further. Keep your cap under
your arm as far as I am concerned. I was only trying to see you quite
comfortable. Now. Will you be staying long? Please... Young man...
Old gentleman... Oh well, Spirit, if you like it. What exactly is your
business with me?
Spirit Your welfare!
Scrooge I take that very kindly of you, Spirit. I take it exceedingly kind.
But so far as my own particular welfare is concerned, a good night's
sleep might have done me some good... With a cup of hot tea around
seven, and a nice bit of business to bring off if it wasn't near Christmas.
Spirit Your reclamation, then. Take heed!
Scrooge My ... what exactly...?
Spirit We shall only find it after a long voyage of discovery. Are you
ready to set out with me?
Scrooge Hardly, Spirit. I'm in my night-gown.
Spirit No matter.
Scrooge Where are we going, did you say?
Spirit On a journey.
Scrooge Are we going far...?
Spirit A very long way indeed! As long as your life, Scrooge.
Scrooge There's a nasty wind out there. A sharp sneaping wind. If I might
put on a pair of trousers, and a greatcoat perhaps?
Spirit Trousers and a greatcoat will not be necessary.
Scrooge A pair of boots perhaps?
Spirit Nor boots neither...
Scrooge Just slippers then as I have a nasty cold upon me... How do we
travel exactly? (*He hastily steps into his slippers which are by the bed*)
Spirit Through the air.

Scrooge I'm a mortal man, remember! I'll drop like a stone. And I have a curious fear of high places.

Spirit You'll not fall. If I touch you—there! (*It puts out a hand and touches Scrooge above his heart*) Now rise and walk with me.

Singers   Angels from the realms of glory
                                   Wing your flight o'er all the earth
                                   Ye who sang creation's story
                                   Now proclaim Messiah's birth
                                   Come and worship
                                   Christ the new-born King.
                                   Come and worship,
                                   Worship Christ the new-born King.

                                   Sages, leave your contemplation
                                   Brighter visions beam afar:
                                   Seek the great Desire of Nations
                                   Ye have seen his natal star:
                                   Come and worship
                                   Christ the new-born King.
                                   Come and worship,
                                   Worship Christ the new-born King.

During this carol Scrooge and the Spirit are walking round the stage—going on a long journey

SCENE 8

The ground is covered with snow, gleaming white in the clear winter sunshine

Scrooge and the Spirit rise into the air, and through the window to a high point over roof-tops, which are still misty. Then the roof-tops disappear, the mist clears

The roofs of a small market town appear

Scrooge Good heavens! This is my country. I was a boy here.

Spirit You remember the road?

Scrooge Remember it? I could walk it blindfolded!

Spirit Strange to have forgotten it for so many years. (*He looks closely at Scrooge*) Your lip's trembling. What's that on your cheek? (*He puts out a hand to touch Scrooge's cheek*)

Scrooge (*turning his face away hastily*) On my cheek? Just a pimple. Oh yes, I tell you. A perfectly ordinary—pimple.

Farmfolk   And here is to Dobbin and to his right eye,
                                       Pray God send our master a good Christmas
                                       And a good Christmas pie that we all may
                                       With our wassailing bowl we'll drink to that

Scrooge Who are they?

Spirit These are but shadows of things that have been. They have no consciousness of us.

Scrooge What are they shouting?

Spirit Listen!

The people on the road are singing snatches of a song to each other

Farmfolk   There was an old man, and he had an old cow
                                       And how for to keep her he didn't know how
                                       He built up a barn for to keep his cow warm
                                       And a drop or two of cider will do us no harm
                                       Sing Merry Christmas, Merry Christmas,
                                       And a drop or two of cider will do us no harm

Scrooge (*cupping his ear with his hand*) I can't hear.

SCENE 9

Spirit Not yet. What's a Merry Christmas to you? Out upon Christmas! That's your opinion of the matter, isn't it, Scrooge?

Scrooge I know him!

Child Scrooge appears in a school

Spirit The school isn't altogether empty. There's one lonely boy, forbidden to come home by his father. Stays on and made to work for his keep. You remember?

Scrooge I was alone.

Spirit Not entirely.
Child Scrooge Open Sesame!

The cupboard door opens

*The characters of the stories Scrooge read as a child come out in turn.
Ali Baba with his slave girl, the beautiful Morgiana. Sinbad the Sailor,
and Robinson Crusoe with his fur hat, and his gun and his parrot on his
shoulder*

Scrooge Ali Baba. I remember him and his beautiful slave girl Morgiana,
who helped boil forty robbers in oil! Sound businessman, Ali! Knew the
value of money and took over his brother's shop.
Parrot (*shrieking*) Poor Robin Crusoe! Where've you been, Robin
Crusoe? Poor Robin Crusoe!
Scrooge I remember Old Crusoe. Just as he came to me that afternoon!
The man thought he was dreaming, but he wasn't. It was the parrot
speaking, you know. And Sinbad the survivor. Got the Old Man of the
Sea drunk on a glass of wine and off his back at last! That's the way to
do business! Mind you, I've been the old man on the back of a good
many who came to borrow money!

Man Friday comes running across the classroom

And here comes Friday. Running away from his enemies who were
going to make a stew out of him... Run, Friday. Run! Hallou! Hoop!
Hallou!
( ) **Chorus** To hear Scrooge expending all the earnestness of his nature
on such subjects...
( ) **Chorus** In a most extraordinary voice between laughing and crying.
( ) **Chorus** And to see his heightened and excited face...
( ) **Chorus** Would have been a surprise to his business friends in the
City.

*Robinson Crusoe raises his gun and fires at Friday's unseen pursuers.
Friday kneels before Crusoe in gratitude*

Headmaster (*off; slightly drunkenly*) Scrooge? Are you there, Scrooge?
Stop idling there, boy. There's potatoes here for peeling! We didn't
keep you on at school so you could read books, you know.

Child Scrooge closes his book

The fictional characters hurry back into the cupboard

Child Scrooge Close Sesame!

The cupboard door closes

Headmaster (*off*) Scrooge!

The Child Scrooge leaves the classroom

Scrooge Poor boy... I wish...
Spirit What do you wish?
Scrooge There was a boy singing a Christmas carol. I needn't have
frightened him away.

*A group appears, with the Boy whom Scrooge frightened with the ruler,
singing "God Bless You Merry, Gentlemen"*

Spirit Let us see another Christmas. (*He holds out his hand*)

*The room seems to crumble; bare laths replace a plaster wall. A window
is broken*

Young Scrooge enters

Scrooge That's me also.
Spirit Still alone, after ten Christmasses.
Scrooge Not reading now. Walking up and down in my cage! With other
boys gone home for jolly holidays...

The Headmaster comes into the classroom. He calls

Headmaster Scrooge!

Young Scrooge starts guiltily, half afraid

Your sister to see you, Scrooge.

Fan, Scrooge's younger sister, runs into the classroom and embraces him

Fan Dear brother.
Young Scrooge Fan... Why are you here?
Fan To bring you home, home, home!
Young Scrooge Home, little Fan? That's not possible.
Fan Yes, it is. Home for good and all. Home forever and forever. Our father has grown much kinder and now home's changed. Home's like heaven. He spoke gently to me when I was going to bed. So I dared ask him if you might come home. And he said "Yes". My dear brother. "Yes, you may". So I've been sent in a coach to bring you.
Young Scrooge (*looking at her with admiration*) You're quite a woman, now. Little Fan.
Fan And you're to be a man—and never come back here again.

Up stage, we see the back of a coach

Headmaster (*shouting*) Fetch down Master Scrooge's box.

An aged servant enters, staggering under the weight of Master Scrooge's trunk

The Headmaster pours out two diminutive glasses of sherry and a large glass for himself. The servant heaves the trunk on the back of the coach

Fan (*to Young Scrooge*) We're to be together all the Christmas long—and have the merriest time in the world.
Headmaster (*still slightly drunk*) You are to be launched, Scrooge, on the dangerous seas of life. Away from this cosy and kindly establishment where you have long been protected and cosseted by the loving hands of self and staff. But however you travel, Scrooge, to whatever distant part of the Empire, beneath what tropic sun or desert cold, you will always feel, in your heart, loyalty and gratitude to this great school which has long given you succour, sir, and been your world! You will remember.
Young Scrooge I promise you, yes!
Headmaster I see I have touched your heart. Your loyal spirit...
Young Scrooge I promise you never to remember you! Never think of you again. Not if I can possibly help it. Come on, Fan.

Music

Beloved eye, beloved star,
Thou art so near and yet so far;
Beloved eye, beloved star,
Thou art so near and yet so far!

Spirit Always a delicate creature, your sister Fan. But she had a great
heart.

Scrooge So she had. I won't deny that. God forbid.

Spirit She died a woman. With, I think, children.

Scrooge One child.

Spirit Your nephew!

Scrooge (*uneasily*) Yes, Fred.

Carol Singers   God bless the master of this house,
And all that are within,
And to begin this Christmas-tide,
With mirth now let us sing.

And this new Christmas carol
Let us cheerfully sing,
To the honour and glory
Of our heavenly King;
And this new Christmas carol
Let us cheerfully sing,
To the honour and glory
Of our heavenly King.

SCENE 10

Scrooge and the Spirit watch as the country turns into a city

*Carol Singers of various appearance mill about. They stop in front of a
warehouse office door with "Fezziwig and Company" written over it.
They sing their carol outside this door*

Spirit You know this place?

Scrooge Know it? Weren't I apprenticed here?

Mr Fezziwig comes out of his front door. He is short, fat, perpetually smiling, wearing a wig, a flowered waistcoat, old fashioned knee breeches, stockings, and buckled shoes. He hands out money to the Carol Singers

The Carol Singers wish him a Merry Christmas. He throws handfuls of sweets—biscuits, etc., which the children catch

Why, it's old Fezziwig, bless his heart! Fezziwig is alive again!

Fezziwig goes through his front door as the Carol Singers depart and we are in his warehouse

A big space with a counter and a tall desk, at which Fezziwig now sits. There are sacks and packing cases and tall shutters

Fezziwig (*calling out in his rich voice*) Seven o'clock. Yo, ho, there! Ebenezer! Dick!

Young Scrooge and Dick Wilkins, both apprentices of about the same age, come in together

Scrooge Dick Wilkins, I dare swear it is! Very much attached to me was poor Dick Wilkins. What? Dear me, yes.
Fezziwig Yo, ho, my boys. So there you are. No more work tonight. It's Christmas Eve, Dick. Christmas is coming, Ebenezer. So what do we do first, this Christmas Eve, eh, boys?
Young Scrooge Have the shutters up, Mr Fezziwig.
Fezziwig Shutters up, Ebenezer. Before a man can say Jack Robinson!

Young Scrooge and Dick Wilkins run round banging the shutters up very fast and letting down the bars to fasten them. They come panting back for full instructions

(*He skips down from his tall desk with great agility*) Hilli-ho! Clear away, my lads, and let's have plenty of room here. Hilli-ho, Dick! Chirrup, Ebenezer!

Young Scrooge and Dick Wilkins clear away sacks, packing cases, etc.

Dick Wilkins Clear away!

Scrooge There's nothing we wouldn't clear away. With old Fezziwig looking on.

Fezziwig Every movable moved away, my lads.

Young Scrooge (*to Dick Wilkins*) As though it's dismissed from public life forever...

Fezziwig Floor swept... Logs on the fire... Lamps trimmed...

The room is transformed as Young Scrooge and Dick Wilkins rush round it. Then, a moment of stillness as they look at the results of their work

Well done, lads! Welcome to the Fezziwig Ball Room and Grand Palace of the Dance. (*He claps his hands*) Bring on the music.

An elderly Fiddler comes in, and arranges his music on the high desk

Scrooge I remember—the old fellow who made an orchestra of Fezziwig's desk.

The Fiddler starts tuning up a painful noise

(*Wincing*) And tuned up like fifty stomach aches.

Fezziwig So, lads. Let the revelry commence!

Mrs Fezziwig enters, dressed in a crinoline

Mrs Fezziwig In comes Mrs Fezziwig, one vast, substantial smile.

The Three Daughters enter

The Three Daughters In comes the three Misses Fezziwigs, beaming and lovable.

Six Young Men enter sighing

Six Young Men In comes the six young followers, whose hearts they broke.

The Housemaid and the Baker enter

Housemaid In comes the housemaid.

Baker With her cousin the baker.

The Cook and the Milkman enter

Cook In comes the cook...
Milkman With her brother's particular friend, the milkman.

A Girl, and a Boy, who is trying to hide himself behind her, enter

Girl In comes the girl from next door, who was thought to have had her ears pulled by her mistress.
Boy Trying to hide behind her is the 'prentice boy from next door but one...
Fezziwig Who is suspected of not getting enough to eat from his master...

The Cook brings in a groaning table of food and drink

Fezziwig looks at it with pride

So Hilli-ho. With our cake and our negus. With our cold roast and our cold boiled. With our minced pies and our beer. With our fiddler. (*He points to the Fiddler*)

The Fiddler bows

An artful dog. The sort of lad who knows his business better than you or I could have told it to him. Shall our Christmas ever die?
All Never die!
Fezziwig Then let dancing commence!

The Fiddler starts to play. The dancing starts. Scrooge leaves his high position, with the Spirit. Then he appears among the dancers, none of whom notice him. He moves towards the audience

Scrooge I remember...
( ) **Chorus** They all dance——
( ) **Chorus** —some shyly——
( ) **Chorus** —some boldly, some gracefully——
( ) **Chorus** —some awkwardly——
( ) **Chorus** —some pushing——

( ) **Chorus** —some pulling.
( ) **Chorus** And off they all go, hand in hand,——
( ) **Chorus** —in the middle and out again,——
( ) **Chorus** —round and round in various stages of affection.
( ) **Chorus** And then all turning up in the wrong place.

The dance has got into a state of confusion and the music stops

Fezziwig (*clapping his hands*) Well done! Let supper commence!

The guests go to the table and start eating. The Fiddler plunges his face in a great tankard

( ) **Chorus** The Fiddler plunges his face into a pot of porter, especially provided for that purpose.
( ) **Chorus** And when the fiddler...
( ) **Chorus** An artful dog, mind!
( ) **Chorus** The sort of man who knows his business better than you or I could have told it to him.
Fezziwig Strikes up "Sir Roger de Coverley"...

The Fiddler plays "Sir Roger"; the guests line up for the dance

( ) **Chorus** Then old Fezziwig stands out to dance with Mrs Fezziwig.
( ) **Chorus** Top couple, too!
( ) **Chorus** With a good stiff piece of work cut out for them.
( ) **Chorus** Three or four and twenty pair of partners.
( ) **Chorus** People who are not to be trifled with!
( ) **Chorus** People who will dance.

The dancing starts. Scrooge gets involved with the dancers

( ) **Chorus** And have no notion of walking.
( ) **Chorus** But if they had been twice as many.
( ) **Chorus** Or four times.
( ) **Chorus** Old Fezziwig would have been a match for them.
( ) **Chorus** And so would Mrs Fezziwig.
( ) **Chorus** As to *her*, she is worthy to be his partner in every sense of the term.

( ) **Chorus** And if that's not high praise, tell me another. And I'll use it!
Scrooge I remember...
( ) **Chorus** A primitive light appears to issue from Fezziwig's calves.
( ) **Chorus** They shine in every part of the dance like moons.
( ) **Chorus** You couldn't predict, at any time, what would become of them next.
( ) **Chorus** And when old Fezziwig and Mrs Fezziwig have gone through the dance...
( ) **Chorus** Advance and retire, hold hands with your partner, bow and curtsey, corkscrew, thread the needle and back again to your place.
( ) **Chorus** Fezziwig cuts so deftly that he appears to wink with his legs and come upon his feet again without a stagger.

Scrooge disappears again among the dancers; we see him occasionally and then he is gone

The clock strikes eleven. The dancing stops. Mr and Mrs Fezziwig stand on each side of the door to say goodbye to the guests, shaking hands with them, wishing them a happy Christmas

( ) **Chorus** Mr and Mrs Fezziwig take their stations.
( ) **Chorus** One on either side of the door.
( ) **Chorus** And shaking hands with every person individually as he or she goes out.
( ) **Chorus** Wish him or her a "Merry Christmas".
( ) **Chorus** When everyone has retired but the two apprentices.
( ) **Chorus** They do the same to them.
Fezziwig Hidi. Ho. Well done, boys. Chirrup. And a Merry Christmas!

Mr and Mrs Fezziwig exit

Dick Wilkins and Young Scrooge are left alone together and get ready for bed

Scrooge reappears beside the Spirit

( ) **Chorus** And thus the cheerful voices die away.
( ) **Chorus** And the lads are left to their beds.
( ) **Chorus** Which are under a counter in the back shop.

Spirit A small matter, isn't it? To give a party and make all those folk so
full of happiness.
Scrooge Small!
Spirit Listen.

*Young Scrooge and Dick Wilkins open two cupboards, under the counter
where their beds are. They start to undress*

Young Scrooge Dear old Fezziwig! We're lucky to work for him, Dick.
Dick Wilkins Who else could make the boy, from next door but one,
cheerful?
Young Scrooge Or get the cook skipping as high as the moon?
Dick Wilkins Or have the Baker, who never smiles, laughing fit to burst
his breeches.
Young Scrooge And turn this old warehouse into a Palace of the Dance?
Dick Wilkins God bless old Fezziwig!
Young Scrooge Yes, Dick. Bless his old heart...
Spirit He's spent a little of your mortal money. Three or four pounds
perhaps. Is that such a wonderful thing to do?
Scrooge It's not the money, Spirit.
Spirit (*looking at him incredulously*) Did *you* say ... it's not the money?
Scrooge He had the power to make us 'prentices happy or miserable. His
power lay in small things, in words and looks which you couldn't add
or count up in a ledger. The happiness he gave was quite as great as if
it cost a fortune.
Dick Wilkins Ebenezer, old fellow.
Young Scrooge Yes, Dick?
Dick Wilkins When we grow old...
Young Scrooge You mean, grow older?
Dick Wilkins We'll still be good friends, will we not?
Young Scrooge I think so...
Dick Wilkins And still have a feast and music and all that laughter at
Christmas? Just like old Fezziwig?
Young Scrooge (*yawning*) Just like him.
Dick Wilkins We're lucky fellows, aren't we?
Young Scrooge So we are. Sleep well.
Dick Wilkins If we could skip and dance like him. When we're quite
old...
Young Scrooge And a Merry Christmas...

Scrooge looks sadly down from his place with the Spirit

Spirit What's the matter?
Scrooge Nothing particular.
Spirit Something, I think.
Scrooge No... No. I should like to be able to say a word or two to my clerk. Just now. That's all.

Dick Wilkins and Young Scrooge get into their cupboard beds and shut the doors

The warehouse is lost in darkness

Spirit My time grows short. Quick!
( ) **Chorus** This was not addressed to Scrooge, or to any one whom he could see, but it produced an immediate effect. For again Scrooge saw himself. He was older now; a man in the prime of his life. His face had not the harsh and rigid lines of later years; but it had begun to wear the signs of care and avarice. There was an eager, greedy, restless motion in the eye, which showed the passion that had taken root, and where the shadow of the growing tree would fall.

SCENE 11

Part of a drawing-room

Young Scrooge is sitting on a couch. A beautiful woman, Belle, is standing, nervous but determined. Young Scrooge is now assured, confident, settled in his beliefs

Young Scrooge You don't understand business, Belle.
Belle Do I not?
Young Scrooge If those idlers don't pay their rents... Why then, they must be put out on the street. I have always paid on the nail!
Belle And collected on the nail too, Ebenezer?
Young Scrooge So I must: am I a charitable organisation? Will we not have expenses? When we have a home together?
Belle No. Ebenezer. It must be no.

Young Scrooge You can't be expected to understand business.

Belle I understand that we can never have a home together.

Young Scrooge (*disbelieving*) Belle?

Belle It will matter little. To you, very little! Another idol has displaced me. If it can cheer and comfort you in time to come—as I would have tried to do—well then, I have no just cause to grieve.

Young Scrooge What idol has displaced you?

Belle A golden one.

Young Scrooge Is this the fair dealing of the world? It's so hard on poverty and yet it condemns wealth... Is that fair of you, Belle?

Belle You are too much afraid of the world. You want to be rich so the world cannot touch you. That's your master passion now. All else is forgotten.

Young Scrooge Perhaps I've become wise at last. But I've not changed towards you!

Belle shakes her head

(*He stands and goes to her*) Have I, Belle?

Belle We used to agree long ago. When we thought you'd work hard and improve our position... Just a little ... and then we'd marry...

Young Scrooge I was a boy then! I was entirely ignorant of business!

Belle And you have changed?

Young Scrooge Not towards you.

Belle When we agreed we were one heart! Now we are two, our agreement is fraught with misery. I won't say how often I have thought I must tell you this. It's enough I have thought it.

Young Scrooge Have I ever tried to wriggle out of our bargain, Belle?

Belle Not in words.

Young Scrooge In what then?

Belle In a changed nature. In an altered spirit. In everything that made my love valuable to you. Tell me honestly. If we had never met before, would you try and win me now—a girl without money, or the hope of money?

Young Scrooge You think not?

Belle I would think otherwise if I could. But now you weigh everything by gain. And if you were false to your new idol and took me ... what repentance and regret would surely follow? (*She moves away from him*) So. Now I must release you from your promise. I do so with a full heart.

For the love of him you once were. (*She moves away further*) Yes. I remember what you were and that makes me think … you may have some pain in this. But soon, very soon you will recover. You will dismiss the memory of me. You'll do it gladly. I was no more than an unprofitable dream. You will be grateful that I woke you up at last. Goodbye, now… May you be happy in the life you have chosen.

She goes into the shadows

Young Scrooge stands alone and then the drawing-room darkens

Scrooge Spirit. Show me no more! Conduct me home! Why do you delight to torture me?
Spirit One shadow more…
Scrooge No more! No more! I will not see it. I will *not*! Show me no more.

Lights up on a couch

> A young mother, Belle's Daughter, is sitting there, surrounded by children who are playing, climbing on her lap, and climbing on the lap of Belle, who we now see also on the couch, wearing a shawl and a cap. A small child climbs on to Belle's lap—and tries to pull off her cap

Belle's Daughter Henrietta! Stop it, Henrietta. Stop tormenting your grandmother.
Belle I don't mind it. My dear, you know I don't mind it at all.

Sound of a door

First Child It's Grandpa. I know it's Grandpa.
Second Child What's he brought us?
Belle's Daughter You spoil them, Father! You've brought them far too much.

Belle's Husband comes in with his arms full of parcels

Belle's Husband Never too much! It's Christmas. Belle… My dearest!

Belle rises. They kiss

The children start to pillage him. They climb on stairs, and unwrap parcels. Laughter. Cries of delight. Belle and her daughter are laughing. Belle's Husband puts his arm round their daughter

Spirit Look at them, Scrooge! Those children, that daughter might have been a spring time in the haggard winter of your life. Now listen.
Belle's Husband Belle. I saw an old friend of yours this afternoon.
Belle Who was it?
Belle's Husband Guess!
Belle How can I? Tut. I don't know. (*She starts to laugh*) Mr Scrooge?
Belle's Husband (*laughing with her*) Mr Scrooge! I passed his office window. He had a candle inside and I could scarcely help seeing him. His partner lies at the point of death I hear. He sat there alone. All quite alone in the world, I do believe.

Light fades on the drawing-room

SCENE 12

Scrooge Spirit! Remove me from this place!
Spirit I told you. These are shadows of things that have been. They are what they are. Don't blame me!
Scrooge Remove me. How can I bear it?
( ) **Chorus** He turns upon the ghost, and seeing it look upon him with a face in which, in some strange way…
( ) **Chorus** There are fragments of all the faces it has shown him. He wrestles with it!
Scrooge Leave me! Take me back! Haunt me no longer!

As Scrooge struggles with the Spirit, the stage is filled with small groups, singing snatches of a carol, quietly

Singers   Saints before the altar bending,
                           Watching long in hope and fear,
                           Suddenly the Lord, descending,
                           In his temple shall appear:
                           Come and worship
                           Christ the new-born King;

> Come and worship
> Worship Christ the new-born King.
>
> Mild, he lays his glory by,
> Born that man no more may die,
> Born to raise the sons of earth,
> Born to give them second birth.
> Hail the heaven-born prince of peace
> Hail the Son of Righteousness!
> Light and life to all he brings,
> Risen with healing in his wings.
>
> Hark! the herald angels sing:
> Glory to the new-born King!

( ) **Chorus** He's conscious of being exhausted.

Scrooge's bed appears. The carol singing swells triumphantly

( ) **Chorus** He gives the cap a parting squeeze.
( ) **Chorus** And has barely time to reel into bed...
( ) **Chorus** Before he sinks into a heavy sleep...

Scrooge falls into the bed and pulls the curtains shut. Sudden darkness and silence

CURTAIN

ACT II

Scene 1

Scrooge's bedroom

Singers

Silent night! holy night!
Sleeps the earth, calm and quiet;
Lovely Child, now take thy rest:
On thy mother's gentle breast
Sleep in heavenly peace!
Sleep in heavenly peace!

Silent night! holy night!
Shepherds first with delight
Heard the angelic "Alleluia!"
Echoing loud, both near and far:
"Jesus, the Saviour, is here!
Jesus, the Saviour, is here!"

( ) **Chorus** Gentlemen of the free and easy sort, getting up of a morning...

( ) **Chorus** Frequently observe that they are good for anything from pitch-and-toss to manslaughter.

( ) **Chorus** Without going as far as that, old Scrooge is fit for any sort of surprises...

( ) **Chorus** After what he's gone through...

( ) **Chorus** And nothing between a baby and a rhinoceros can astonish him. Very much.

( ) **Chorus** Now, being prepared for anything, he is not by any means prepared for nothing!

The clock strikes one

( ) **Chorus** Consequently, when the bell strikes one, and no shape appears...

Red Light concentrates and grows stronger on Scrooge's bed

( ) **Chorus** He is taken with a violent fit of trembling.
( ) **Chorus** Five minutes.
( ) **Chorus** Ten minutes.
( ) **Chorus** A quarter of an hour goes by.
( ) **Chorus** Yet nothing comes.
( ) **Chorus** All this time Scrooge lies upon his bed.
( ) **Chorus** The very core and centre of a blaze of ruddy light.
( ) **Chorus** Which, being the only light, is more alarming than a dozen ghosts.
( ) **Chorus** He is powerless to make out what it means.
( ) **Chorus** And is somehow apprehensive that he may be an interesting case of spontaneous combustion!
( ) **Chorus** At last, however, he begins to think that the source and secret of this ghostly light might be in another room.
( ) **Chorus** The idea taking full possession of his mind...
( ) **Chorus** He gets up softly.
( ) **Chorus** And shuffles in his slippers to the door.

Scrooge tiptoes down the stairs. A deep voice calls him

Spirit Of Christmas Present (*off*) Scrooge!
Scrooge (*resignedly*) Another spirit. I don't doubt it.
Spirit (*off*) Come down here and know me better! Scrooge!

Scrooge opens a door at the foot of the stairs, into a room flooded with red light

> *We see the Spirit of Christmas Present. It is large, strong, cheerful, wearing a deep green robe bordered with white fur which leaves its chest bare. Its feet are also bare. On its head is a holly wreath, glittering with icicles. It is girded with a belt from which hangs a rusty scabbard, which contains no sword. It carries a torch and is sitting on a throne among holly and mistletoe and piles of chickens, turkeys, fruit and a steaming bowl of punch*

The space is lit as though with the glow of a huge and cheerfully blazing fire

I am the Ghost of Christmas Present! You've never seen the like of me
before?

Scrooge Never in my life.

Spirit Never walked out with my young brothers? They are older than me,
for I am very young.

Scrooge I can't say I have. Do you have a *large* family, Spirit?

Spirit More than eighteen hundred. One born every year ... since the first.

Scrooge That's a prodigious large family for a man to support!

The Spirit rises from the couch

Spirit, conduct me where you will. I went forth last night on compulsion,
and learnt a lesson which is working now. Tonight, if you have anything
to teach me, let me profit by it! But don't you be hard on me. Not too
terribly hard, eh? How do we travel exactly?

Spirit Through the air.

Scrooge I am a mortal man, remember. I'll drop like a stone, and I have
a curious fear of heights.

Spirit Touch my robe.

Music: "All Hail to the Days"

Scrooge and the Spirit rise in the air, into the darkness

*The red Light, the decorations and Scrooge's bedroom become dark also.
Sound of spades scraping away snow*

SCENE 2

Singers   All hail to the days that merit more praise
                               Than all the rest of the year,
                               And welcome the nights that double delights
                               As well for the poor as the peer!
                               Good fortune attend each merry man's friend
                               That doth but the best that he may,
                               Forgetting old wrongs with carols and songs,
                               To drive the cold winter away,
                               To drive the cold winter away.

( ) **Chorus** White snow on the roof-tops!
( ) **Chorus** Dirtier snow on the ground below!
( ) **Chorus** Ploughed in deep furrows that cross and recross each other hundreds of times.
( ) **Chorus** There's nothing very cheerful in the climate or the town.
( ) **Chorus** And yet there's a lot of cheerfulness abroad.
Singers   'Tis ill for a mind to anger inclined
                                 To think of small injuries now;
                                 If wrath be to seek, do not lend her thy cheek,
                                 Nor let her inhabit thy brow.
                                 Old grudges forgot are put in the pot,
                                 All sorrows aside they lay;
                                 The old and the young doth carol this song,
                                 To drive the cold winter away,
                                 To drive the cold winter away.
( ) **Chorus** The poulterers' shops are still half open.
( ) **Chorus** The fruiterers are still radiant in their glory.

The Chorus put down the spades and hurry to the shops where fruit and food are set in great piles

( ) **Chorus** There are great, round, pot-bellied buckets of chestnuts, shaped like the waistcoats of jolly old gentlemen.
( ) **Chorus** There are ruddy, brown faced, broad-girthed onions, shining in the fatness of their growth like Spanish Friars——
( ) **Chorus** —and winking in wanton shyness at the girls...
( ) **Chorus (Girl)** As they go by, glancing demurely at the hung-up mistletoe.
( ) **Chorus** And oh, the grocers ... nearly closed.
( ) **Chorus** With the canisters rattling up and down like juggling tricks.
( ) **Chorus** (*sniffing*) And the blended scents of tea and coffee so grateful to the nose!
( ) **Chorus** And the raisins so plentiful and rare!
( ) **Chorus (Child)** And the candied fruits so caked and spotted with molten sugar as to make the coldest looker-on feel faint——
( ) **Chorus** —and subsequently bilious.
( ) **Chorus** And the customers so eager that they tumble up against each other and clash their wicker baskets and leave their purchases behind.
( ) **Chorus** And make all such mistakes in the best humour possible.

Church bells, then a sound of a distant organ

( ) **Chorus** Now all the good people are called to church or chapel.

The children are being called, tidied up, having their caps forced on, families troop off to church

   Bob Cratchit and Tiny Tim appear and go off to church with the others

( ) **Chorus** Other good people filled the Baker's shop to get their Christmas dinner cooked.

   More people appear with their dinners under covers and troop into the Baker's shop

The Spirit is looking at them carefully

( ) **Chorus** The sight of these poor revellers seemed to interest the Spirit very much.

   People are coming out of the Baker's shop with their dinners cooked

The Spirit lifts the covers and looks at the steaming birds and joints. It sprinkles them with sparks from his torch and puts the covers back on them

   A man and a woman come out of the Baker's shop and collide. They shout angrily at each other

   Two small children—who we'll see later are the young Cratchits— come out of the bakery

The Spirit lifts the cover off their dish, reveals a very small goose, and sprinkles it

   The small Cratchits carry it off

Scrooge Would you apply your charms to any kind of dinner on this day?
Spirit To any kindly given. To a poor one most.
Scrooge Why to a poor one most?

Spirit Because it needs it most… Come!

Scrooge holds the Spirit's robe

The Spirit shakes its torch, emitting a shower of sparks. The house and shops are gone

Scrooge and the Spirit are gone with them

SCENE 3

The Cratchits' kitchen

Mrs Cratchit, dressed in her poor best, with bright ribbons, is laying the table. Her daughter, Belinda, helps her. Peter Cratchit, a teenager who is almost lost in a huge wing collar of his father's, plunges a fork into a pot of potatoes

Peter (*shouting*) They're not boiling yet, Mother! (*He puts a lid on the saucepan*)

Mrs Cratchit Whatever's happened to your father and Tim? And Martha? Martha wasn't even late last Christmas.

Peter blows up the fire under the potatoes. There is a shower of sparks over the stage

The Spirit and Scrooge appear above and the Spirit shakes the torch over the Cratchit household

Martha comes into the kitchen. She is the oldest of the Cratchit children

Where's Martha?

Martha Here's Martha, Mother…

Peter And here's the potatoes boiling at last. All ready for the goose.

Martha We were up past eleven sewing a ballgown for a lady. And then we had to be up early to clean the shop for Christmas.

Mrs Cratchit Never mind that, so long as you've come. Sit you down before the fire, my dear, and have a warm, Lord bless you!

Martha Thank goodness. I can have a rest tomorrow.
Mrs Cratchit Your father can't. He has to be up early.

*During Martha's speech that follows, Bob Cratchit appears outside the
door, carrying Tiny Tim and his crutch, cantering as though he were a
spirited horse and Tiny Tim were his rider*

Martha That's too bad. Why has he? I know why. (*She purses her lips*)
Mr Scrooge!
Belinda That's Father coming! Hide, Martha.

*Martha hides in a broom cupboard. Bob Cratchit comes on, carrying Tiny
Tim. He looks round, disappointed*

Bob Cratchit Where's our Martha?
Mrs Cratchit Not coming!
Bob Cratchit (*putting Tiny Tim down*) Not coming! That's spoilt half our
Christmas.
Martha No. It won't, Father. (*She bursts out of the cupboard, throws her
arms round Bob, and kisses him*) Come on, Tim. Come and see how the
pudding is bubbling...

Martha takes Tiny Tim out by the hand

Peter pokes the potatoes again with a fork

Mrs Cratchit And how did little Tim behave in church, Bob?
Bob Cratchit Good as gold! Even better. But he comes out with the
strangest things... On the way home he said he hoped people saw him
in church because he was a cripple. It might be pleasant for them to
remember who made lame beggars walk and blind men see...

Mrs Cratchit looks sad. Bob puts his arm round her

But our Tim's growing stronger each day, isn't he? Each day he grows
more hearty.

Sound of Tiny Tim's cough

Tiny Tim comes back with Martha and stands by the fire

At the same time the young Cratchits come running in with the goose under its cover

Young Cratchits The goose! The goose!
Peter (*taking the dish from them*) The goose. Make way for the goose!

Peter starts a procession round the table. He marches round, followed by the rest of the family, holding knives like drawn swords. The Chorus surround the house, and peer in at the windows. They sniff appreciatively. Then Peter puts the goose down in front of Mrs Cratchit's place. Mrs Cratchit takes off the cover. They shout "Hurrah for the goose". Then they start work frantically

Mrs Cratchit Mrs Cratchit makes the gravy hissing hot!
Peter Master Peter mashes the potatoes with incredible vigour.
Belinda Miss Belinda sweetens up the apple sauce.
Martha Martha dusts the hot plates.
First Young Cratchit And the young Cratchits set chairs for everybody.
Second Young Cratchit Not forgetting themselves, and they cram spoons into their mouths.
Peter Lest they should shriek for "goose" before their turn comes to be served.

The food is on the table, the family are in their places and there is a moment of silence

Bob Cratchit For what we are about to receive, may the Lord makes us truly thankful.

In the silence, Mrs Cratchit, in a breathless pause, looks down at the carving knife like a fencer. Then she plunges it in. All the family sigh with pleasure. Tiny Tim, sitting next to Bob, beats on the table with the handle of his knife

Mrs Cratchit serves out the goose

I don't believe there was such a goose cooked before!
Mrs Cratchit Not for tenderness, size and cheapness!
Martha And enough for all!

Peter Eked out by the apple sauce ... and potatoes mashed by me!

Martha What a goose!

Scrooge Spirit! Tell me if Tiny Tim will live.   *Concerned*

Spirit If these shadows are not altered, he will die.

Scrooge No, no. Kind spirit. Let him live...

Spirit I said if those shadows are not altered, none of my kind, who come after me, will see him there. What of that? Does that concern you, Scrooge? Remember your own words. If he'd like to die, he'd better get on with it and reduce the surplus population.   *disdain*

Scrooge Shouldn't never have said that!

Spirit Man! Forbear that wicked cant. Will you decide what men shall live? What men should die? In the sight of heaven it may be you are more worthless and less fit to live than millions like this poor man's child. Oh God! Spare us from hearing the insect on the leaf deciding there's too much life among his hungry brothers in the dust!

Mrs Cratchit (*tearfully*) The pudding, suppose it's not done enough...

Mrs Cratchit goes out to get the pudding

Belinda (*calling after her*) Suppose it breaks up when you turn it out.

Peter (*calling after her*) Suppose someone climbed over the back wall and stole it!

Young Cratchits (*together*) Hooroo!

Mrs Cratchit comes back with the flaming pudding—rather small

Martha There it is, safe and sound!

Mrs Cratchit (*putting it down and serving it out*) I had a moment of uncertainty—about the quantity of flour!

Bob Cratchit Never you fear. It's a wonderful pudding. If I may speak without exaggeration, Mrs Cratchit, I must regard this pudding as the single greatest achievement of our married life! Now. (*He looks round the table*) Merry Christmas to us all. God bless us.

The family repeat "God bless us". Then we hear Tiny Tim's voice in a moment of silence

Tiny Tim God bless us everyone.

Fade out the Lights

Lights up in the Cratchit kitchen. The family have left the table and are sitting round a steaming bowl of punch. Bob Cratchit is standing with a glass in his hand

Bob Cratchit I'll give you, one and all, the good health of Mr Scrooge. The founder of the feast.

Mrs Cratchit The founder of the feast indeed! I wish I had him here! I'd give him a piece of my mind to feast on, and I hope he'd have a good appetite for it!

Bob Cratchit (*protesting*) My dear! The children! Christmas Day!

Mrs Cratchit It should be Christmas Day, I'm sure, on which one drinks the health of such an odious, stingy, hard, unfeeling man as Mr Scrooge.

Scrooge Is it me she speaks of?

Spirit It's what she knows...

Mrs Cratchit And you know it too, Robert. Nobody know it better than you, poor fellow.

Bob Cratchit Remember, my dear. Christmas.

Mrs Cratchit I'll drink his health for your sake, and the day's sake. Not for his. A Merry Christmas and a Happy New Year—he'll be very merry and very happy, I don't doubt.

Others Mr Scrooge.

The family drink Scrooge's health with a marked lack of enthusiasm

Bob Cratchit And the news I have for you, young Peter, is—you are offered a junior clerkship at the most respectable company with whom Mr Scrooge does business at a salary of ... wait for it! Full five shillings and sixpence by the week. Which, in all the circumstances, I consider princely.

Martha Princely, indeed!

Belinda What are you going to do with all that money, Peter?

Mrs Cratchit No doubt he'll invest it on the Stock Exchange. As Mr Scrooge does his, won't you, Peter?

Bob Cratchit So here's to Master Peter. In his new position. Master Peter. And now. It gives me great pleasure to call on the youngest of the Cratchits ... to entertain the company in song!

Tiny Tim stands and sings "If Bethlehem Were Here Today"

Tiny Tim   If Betlehem were here today
                                 Just as it was before,

I'd run down to the stable bare
And quietly push the door;
And mother holds my hand and smiles
And whispers, "now, take care"—
I'd gently kiss the little boy
And touch His golden hair.
While Mary puts the blankets back
And gentle talk begin,
I'd tiptoe very gently out
And meet the wise men going in.

During his singing, the Light begins to fade on the Cratchits' home, but the Spirit sprinkles a Light on Tiny Tim

Spirit A fortunate family!
Scrooge Why do you say that? Their shoes look far from waterproof. And their clothes, scanty.
Spirit True! They're not handsome, nor well dressed.—
Scrooge And that young Peter's seen the inside of a pawn shop. I dare swear it...
Spirit But learn this from them, Scrooge! They are pleased with one another, and contented with the time...

The Light on the family is fading. It is brightest on Tiny Tim. Then the Light on Tiny Tim, and his song, fades completely

SCENE 4

The Chorus come on

Spirit Hold your gown about you, Scrooge! We're going on a journey.
Scrooge Where to exactly?
Spirit You'll discover soon enough.
Child Solo   While shepherds watched their flocks by night
All seated on the ground
The angel of the lord came down
And glory shone around.

All glory be to God on high
And to the earth be peace;

Goodwill henceforth from heaven to men
Begin and never cease.

( ) Chorus And now, without a word of warning from the Spirit, they stand upon a bleak and deserted moor. Down in the West, the setting sun leaves a streak of fiery red which gazes upon the desolation for an instant, like a sullen eye and frowning lower and lower yet, is lost in the thick gloom of darkest night.

Old Man O master and missus, O are you all within?
Pray open the door and let us come in.
O master and missus a-sitting by the fire.
Pray think upon poor travellers a-travelling in the mire.

Scrooge What place is this?

Spirit A place where miners live. They labour in the bowels of the earth, but they know me. See!

( ) Chorus A light shines through the window of a hut, and swiftly they advance towards it!

Old Man | *(together)* For it's your wassail, and it's our wassail,
Children | And it's joy be to you, and a jolly wassail.
For it's your wassail, and it's our wassail,
And it's joy be to you, and a jolly wassail.

Old Man O where is the maid with the silver-headed pin
To open the door and let us come in?
O master and missus, o it is our desire
For a good loaf and cheese and a toast by the fire!

( ) Chorus Passing through the wall of mud and stone they find a cheerful company assembled round glowing fire. All decked out gaily in their holiday attire. The old man is singing them a Christmas song. It had been a very old song when he was a boy and from time to time they all join in the chorus:

Family For it's your wassail, and it's our wassail,
And it's joy be to you, and a jolly wassail.

Company For it's your wassail, and it's our wassail,
And it's joy be to you, and a jolly wassail.

( ) Chorus So surely as they raise their voices the old man gets quite blithe and loud. (*He pauses*) The Spirit does not tarry there, but bids Scrooge hold his robe. And passing on above the moor … speeds…

Company I saw three ships come sailing in

> On Christmas Day, on Christmas Day,
> I saw three ships come sailing in
> On Christmas Day in the morning.

( ) **Chorus** Whither?

Scrooge (*afraid*) Not to sea?

( ) **Chorus** To sea!

Scrooge I was never much of a sailor, Spirit. I don't know as how my stomach will stand it.

Company   And what was in those ships all three
> On Christmas Day, on Christmas Day?
> And what was in those ships all three
> On Christmas Day in the morning?

( ) **Chorus** Scrooge, looking back fearfully, sees the last of the land. (*He pauses*) His ears are deafened by the thundering of water. (*He pauses*) It rolls and roars and rages among the dreadful caverns and tries to undermine the earth.

Company   Our Saviour Christ and His lady
> On Christmas Day, on Christmas Day
> Our Saviour Christ and His lady
> On Christmas Day in the morning.

Scrooge The truth is, Spirit, that my stomach is ever of a nervous disposition...

Company   Then let us all rejoice amain
> On Christmas Day, on Christmas Day.
> Then let us all rejoice amain
> On Christmas Day, on Christmas Day,
> On Christmas Day in the morning.

A beam from a lighthouse is moving across the sky

Old Salt   Our wassail cup is made of the rosemary tree,
> And so is your beer of the best barley!
> Call up the butler of this house, put on his golden
> ring,
> Let him bring us up a glass of beer and better we
> shall sing!

( ) **Chorus** But upon a dreadful reef of sunken rocks, stands a solitary lighthouse. (*He pauses*) And storm birds—born of the wind one might suppose, as seaweed is of the water. (*He pauses*) Rise and fall about it like the waves they skim.

We see the lighthouse men, lit by a fire, drinking and singing at a table

Singers Men love and joy come to you
And to your wassail too,
And God bless you and send you a Happy New
Year too,
And God send you a Happy New Year!

( ) **Chorus** But even here the men who watch the light have made a fire, and wish themselves a "Merry Christmas" in their can of grog and strike up a sturdy song that is gale in itself:

Company Love and joy come to you,
And to you your wassail too,
And God bless you and send you a Happy New
Year too,
And God send you a Happy New Year!

Spirit Come...!
Scrooge Where to now...?
Spirit Far from any shore.

Scrooge and the Spirit move on

( ) **Chorus** Again the ghost speeds on——
Singers Puer nobis nascitur rector angelorum
In hoc mundo pascitur Dominus Dominorum,
Dominus Dominorum.

( ) **Chorus** —above the black and heaving sea until... (*He pauses*) They alight on a ship swaying in the storm.

We see Sailors on deck, a helmsman at a wheel. Scrooge and the Spirit stand beside him

And stand beside the helmsman at the wheel. Every man among them hums a Christmas tune. (*He pauses*) Or has a Christmas thought. (*He pauses*) Or speaks of some bygone Christmas Day. (*He pauses*) With homeward hopes belonging to it.

Company Every voice in quire now blend
To hymn our Saviour source and end:
In sweet concord sing we so:

( ) **Chorus** It is a great surprise to Scrooge, while listening to the moaning of the wind... (*He pauses*) And thinking what a solemn thing

it is to move on through the darkness over an unknown abyss, whose
depths and secrets are as profound as death.

Company   Benedicamus Domino. Benedicamus Domino,
Benedicamus Domino.

( ) **Chorus** It's a great surprise to Scrooge, while thus engaged ... (*He
pauses*) To hear a hearty laugh! (*He pauses*) It's a great surprise to
Scrooge to recognise it as his own nephew's. (*He pauses*) And to find
himself in a bright, dry, gleaming room, with the Spirit standing by his
side. (*He pauses*) And looking at that same nephew with approving
affability!

SCENE 5

Scrooge's Nephew's living room

*A Christmas party. Guests drinking, roasting chestnuts, etc., are gathered
round a big fire. Scrooge's Nephew is standing in front of the fire,
laughing hugely. Among the guests are his pretty young wife, Scrooge's
Niece, a number of the niece's sisters, including her Plump Sister with the
lace tucker, and Topper, the Nephew's bachelor friend. The Chorus are
now guests and the atmosphere is exceedingly jolly. Scrooge and the
Spirit, invisible to other characters, stand outside the group round the fire,
but in the room*

*Scrooge's Nephew is still laughing heartily and the others join in, only
stopping to say their Chorus lines*

( ) **Chorus** If you happen, by some unlikely chance to know a man more
blest in a laugh than Scrooge's nephew...

( ) **Chorus** All I can say is, I should like to know him too.

( ) **Chorus** Introduce me to him and I'll cultivate his acquaintance!

( ) **Chorus** When Scrooge's nephew laughs this way...

( ) **Chorus** Holding his sides, rolling his head and twisting his face into
the most extravagant contortions...

( ) **Chorus** Scrooge's niece, by marriage, laughs as heartily as he!

( ) **Chorus** And their assembled friends, not being a bit behind hand, roar
out lustily.

Nephew As I live! He said that Christmas was a humbug! (*Through the
laughter*) He believes it too!

Niece More shame to him, Fred.

Nephew Scrooge is a comical old fellow! That's the truth. And not pleasant as he might be. But his offences carry their punishment. I have really nothing against him.

Niece And I'm sure he's very rich, Fred. So you always tell me.

Nephew What of that, my dear? His money's no use to him. He don't do any good with it. He don't make himself comfortable with it. He hasn't the satisfaction of thinking— (*Through the laughter*) that he's going to benefit us with it!

Niece I have no patience with him!

Niece's Sisters (*in a Chorus*) Neither have we.

( ) **Chorus** No patience at all, with old Scrooge!

Nephew Oh, I couldn't be angry with him if I tried. Who suffers by his ill tempered whims? Why, no-one but himself. He takes it in his head to dislike us and won't come and dine with us. So what's the consequence? Does he lose much of a dinner?

Niece Indeed, I think he loses a very good dinner!

( ) **Chorus** An excellent dinner.

( ) **Chorus** We know that.

( ) **Chorus** We've eaten it!

( ) **Chorus** So we must be allowed to be the best judges.

Nephew I'm not sure beautiful young brides make good housekeepers. Housekeepers are best, old and strict and fat around the middle. What do you say, Topper?

Topper I say I'm a bachelor. That is to say I'm a wretched outcast.

( ) **Chorus** Topper has clearly got his eye on one of Scrooge's niece's sisters...

( ) **Chorus** The one with the roses on her dress?

( ) **Chorus** No. The plump one with the lace tucker.

Topper So who am I to pass judgement on beautiful young brides?

Niece (*to Nephew*) Go on, Fred. He never finishes what he begins to say. He's such a ridiculous fellow!

Nephew What I was going to say... Before I was rudely interrupted... We should be sorry for Scrooge. He's losing some pleasant moments which can do him no harm. I'm sure he would find better company with us than with his own thoughts. More warmth with us than his mouldy old office, or his dusty rooms. So I mean to give him the chance, and extend the same invitation every year! Whether he likes it or not. He may rail at Christmas as much as he likes but I'll wear him down in the end, I swear I will! And if that puts him in the vein of leaving his poor nephew fifty pounds in his will, that's something. (*He laughs*) I think I shook him yesterday.

The Singers begin a Victorian air

Singers   I know an eye, so softly bright,
                           That glistens like a star of night;
                           My soul it draws with glances kind
                           To heaven's vault, and there I find
                           Another star as pure and clear
                           As that which mildly sparkles here.

                           Beloved eye, beloved star,
                           Thou art so near and yet so far;
                           Beloved eye, beloved star,
                           Thou art so near and yet so far,
                           So near and yet so far.

Scrooge I know that little air! My sister Fan used to sing before I was sent away to school. So many years ago.
Spirit Listen to it, Scrooge. If you remembered it more often you might… I think you might…
Scrooge I might—what? Spirit?
Spirit Have cultivated the kindness in life for your own happiness and with your own hands without resorting to the sexton's spade that buried Jacob Marley!

The Singers continue the air

Niece What's the matter with all of us? Are we to have no games this year?
Nephew (*producing a large handkerchief*) Who will be blind man?

Scrooge produces a handkerchief from his dressing-gown pocket and starts to blindfold himself gleefully

Topper I suppose. As a wretched, outcast of a bachelor… One, two, three…

The Nephew blindfolds Topper, not very effectively, and spins him round. Topper staggers about with his arms outstretched, and the girls run away screaming. Then Topper sets out in pursuit of the niece's Plump Sister

( ) **Chorus** I no more believe Topper is really blind than I believe he has eyes in his boots.

( ) **Chorus** I believe it's all a plot between him and Scrooge's nephew.

The Spirit smiles at this, and nods its head vigorously. We see blindfolded Scrooge running away from the guests and also Topper chasing the Plump Sister

( ) **Chorus** The way he's going after that plump sister in the lace tucker is an outrage to the credulity of human nature!

( ) **Chorus** Knocking down the fire irons! Bumping against the piano! Smothering himself in the curtains. Wherever she goes, there goes he.

( ) **Chorus** He won't catch anyone else!

( ) **Chorus** If you fall against him and stand there, he only makes a faint effort to catch you.

Plump Sister (*crying out*) It isn't fair! It really is not fair.

( ) **Chorus** But for all her rapid flutterings and silken rustlings...

( ) **Chorus** He gets her into a corner from which there is no escape.

( ) **Chorus** His conduct is the most execrable. Pretending not to know her!

( ) **Chorus** Pretending it's necessary to touch her. To assure himself of her identity...

( ) **Chorus** By pressing a certain ring on her finger...

( ) **Chorus** And a certain chain about her neck...

Topper It's Miss Rosee!

( ) **Chorus** What a surprise!

Another guest takes the blindfold from Topper and puts it on. Scrooge takes off his blindfold and returns to stand by the Spirit

( ) **Chorus** Topper's behaviour is vile and monstrous!

The plump niece leads Topper to the window. They go behind the curtains

( ) **Chorus** And no doubt that's why the plump sister is taking Topper behind the curtain.

( ) **Chorus** To tell him how vilely he has behaved!

The game goes on. The Niece sits by the fire. Scrooge and the Spirit stand

behind her. The blind man quickly catches and identifies a girl. The game
stops. The guests gather round the fire again

Niece (*calling out*) Animal, vegetable and mineral!
Spirit (*to Scrooge*) Our time is almost over.
Scrooge But there's a new game starting...
Spirit Very well, then. But only a little while...
Niece It's animal...
Scrooge How many legs?
Guest How many legs?
Niece Er ... well. Two.
Scrooge Can you eat it?
Guest Can you eat it?
Niece Yes.
Guest Can it eat you...?
Niece It might gobble you up.
Scrooge Has it got wings?
Guest Has it got wings?
Niece Yes.
Scrooge It's a turkey!
Nephew Is it a turkey?
Niece Yes!

Universal clapping in which Scrooge joins enthusiastically

Nephew It's animal.
Plump Sister Does it live in a menagerie?
Nephew No.
Guest Is it ever sold in a market?
Nephew No.
Scrooge Is it a horse?
Guest Is it a horse?
Nephew No.
Niece's Sister A dog.
Nephew No.
Niece Is it to be found in London?
Nephew Lives in London. Yes.
Scrooge Savage?
Guest Is it savage?
Nephew Sometimes.

Scrooge Does it growl and grunt?
Niece Does it growl and grunt?
Nephew Yes. Quite often.
Plump Sister Is it an agreeable animal?
Nephew No.
Topper Disagreeable?
Nephew Yes.
Guest When you see it in London—is it led about the streets?
Nephew No.
Guest Is it a bear?
Nephew No. A bear with a sore head perhaps.
Scrooge Is it fight-fisted?
Plump Sister Is it tight-fisted?
Nephew (*laughing*) Exceedingly!
Plump Sister (*calling out laughing*) I've found it out! I know what it is,
    Fred! I know what it is!
Nephew What is it, then?
Plump Sister It is your Uncle Sc——
All (*joining in, including Scrooge*) —ROOOGE!

*Everyone claps. Scrooge joins in cheerfully. Nephew pours out mulled
wine with a ladle*

Nephew He has given us plenty of merriment, that's sure. It would be pure
    ingratitude not to drink his health. So I say a Merry Christmas and a
    Happy New Year to the old man wherever he is! He wouldn't take it
    from us, but he may have done it none the less. So raise your glasses one
    and all. And a toast to Uncle Scrooge.
All Uncle S-C-R-O-O-G-E!

Scrooge starts a speech in reply. They obviously can't hear him

Scrooge My compliments to you all. Each and everyone. On this most
    auspicious... This most joyful occasion... May I propose a toast to my
    nephew and niece—coupled with the names of Mr Topper and the
    Plump Sister, whom I would advise to purchase a small annuity for any
    future member of their family. This might be had at a discount...
Spirit It's no use, Scrooge. They can't hear you. We are invisible, don't
    you remember? And we must go once more up on our travels.

Scrooge and the Spirit go

The Light fades to darkness

( ) **Chorus** That night Scrooge and the Spirit travel far.

SCENE 6

The dark Chorus figures are against a light background. We can see the distant city

( ) **Chorus** Much they see and many hours they visit.
( ) **Chorus** But always with a happy end.
( ) **Chorus** The Spirit stands beside sick children and they are cheerful.
( ) **Chorus** On foreign lands and they are close to home.
( ) **Chorus** By poverty and it is rich.
( ) **Chorus** In alms houses, hospitals and jails, in misery's every refuge.
( ) **Chorus** Where vain man, in his little brief authority, cannot make fast the door and turn the Spirit out...
( ) **Chorus** He leaves his blessing and teaches Scrooge his precepts.
( ) **Chorus** It's a long night if it is only a night; but Scrooge has his doubts of this.
( ) **Chorus** He observes that during their travels the Spirit grows older...
( ) **Chorus** Clearly older. But he never speaks of it.
( ) **Chorus** Until they are leaving a children's "Twelfth Night" party ... and he notices that the Spirit's hair is grey.

Scrooge and the Spirit appear, standing together in an empty space. The Spirit is wearing a voluminous robe

We can see London in the distance

Scrooge Are Spirits' lives so short?
Spirit My life upon this earth is very brief, It ends tonight.
Scrooge Tonight!
Spirit Tonight at midnight.

The chimes ring three quarters

Hark! The time is drawing near.

Scrooge looks closely at the Spirit's feet

Scrooge Forgive me, Spirit, please. If this is not an impertinent question. But I do see something strange, and not belonging to your good self, protruding from your skirts? Is it a foot, perhaps, or a claw?
Spirit It might be a claw, for all the flesh there is upon it. Look here! Oh man, look here, look, look, and down here. (*It opens the voluminous skirts of its gown to reveal:*)

Two wretched, frightful, abject, hideous and miserable children. They kneel at the Spirit's feet, clinging to its robe

Scrooge turns away his eyes in horror and disgust

Oh, man! Look here. Look, look, and down here! *angry*
( ) **Chorus** The children, wretched, abject, frightful, hideous, miserable.

The Chorus, half curious, half reluctant and afraid to look, move closer to the ghastly children, who almost whisper the following lines

( ) **Chorus** A boy and a girl! Yellow, meagre, ragged, scowling, wolfish.
( ) **Chorus** But prostrate too, in their humility.
( ) **Chorus** When graceful youth should have filled their features out...
( ) **Chorus** And touched them with the freshest tints!
( ) **Chorus** A stale, shrivelled hand, like that of age, has pinched and twisted them, and pulled them into shreds.
( ) **Chorus** Where angels might have sat enthroned—devils lurk.
( ) **Chorus** And glare out menacingly!
( ) **Chorus** Through all the mysteries of wonderful creation.
( ) **Chorus** No degradation of humanity...
( ) **Chorus** Has monsters half so horrible and dread.
Spirit What have you to say of this, Scrooge...? *angry*
Scrooge (*trying hard*) They are... I suppose they are weakly fine children. (*He calls out in agony*) Whose are they? Spirit! Are they yours?
Spirit They are Man's! And they cling to me in flight from their fathers. This boy is Ignorance. This girl is Want. Beware them both, and all of their degree, but most of all beware this boy, for on his brow I see that

to audience   A Christmas Carol

written which is Doom, <u>unless the writing be erased.</u> (*It points towards
the City*) Deny it, all you complacent people! Slander those who tell it
ye. Admit it for your factious purposes, and make it worse. And then…
Wait in patience for the end.

Scrooge Have they no refuge? No shelter?

Spirit Are there no prisons? Are there no workhouses? Do you remember
who said that, Scrooge? *answer*

Before Scrooge can answer, the clock starts to strike twelve

As the strokes echo, a mist rises

The Spirit of Christmas Present vanishes

Scrooge looks for it, calling out

Scrooge Spirit! X

SCENE 7

*Scrooge sees a solemn phantom, draped and hooded, gliding like mist
along the ground, towards him. As it approaches, Scrooge kneels, very
much afraid. The phantom is very tall, shrouded in a deep, black habit, like
a monk, with a hood so its face is hidden. All that can be seen is a skeletal
hand pointing on past Scrooge*

Scrooge Am I in the presence of the Spirit of Christmas Yet to Come?

No answer from the Spirit. He is still pointing

You are about to show me shadows of the things that have not happened,
but *will* happen in the time before us? Is that so, Spirit?

*The Spirit inclines its head under the hood. It is still pointing. Scrooge gets
to his feet, trembling*

Ghost of the Future! I fear you more than any of the Spectres I've seen
so far. But I know that your purpose is to do me good. I tell you I hope

to live to be a different man from what I was. I do hope that, Ghost. So
I'm ready to bear you company, and with a thankful heart. But do speak,
I beg you. (*He pauses*) Will you not speak to me?

The Spirit still points and starts to move

Lead on, then! Lead me on. The night is waning fast and it's a precious
time for me. Lead on, Spirit.

*They move towards the City, or it seems to move towards them. Then there
is a clamour on the Stock Exchange figures. Figures and prices are being
shouted, voices chattering. Businessmen in top hats hurry in with lists.
There are boards with share prices. Scrooge and the Spirit, invisible to
them all, move among them*

( ) **Chorus** There they are, in the heart of it!
( ) **Chorus** On 'Change, among the merchants.
( ) **Chorus** Who hurry up and down and chink the money in their
pockets.
( ) **Chorus** And look at their watches.
( ) **Chorus** And toy thoughtfully with their great gold seals.

*The Spirit stops beside a little knot of businessmen. Scrooge stops also and
listens to their conversation eagerly*

First Businessman No, no, nothing! I don't know much about it either
way. I only know he's dead.
Second Businessman When did he die?
First Businessman Last night, I believe.
Third Businessman I thought he'd last forever. What was the matter with
him?
First Businessman (*yawning*) God knows!
Fourth Businessman What has he done with his money!
First Businessman I haven't heard. Left it to his company, suppose. He
had no-one close. He hasn't left a penny to me, that's all I know! (*He
laughs*) It's likely to be a very cheap funeral. Upon my life I don't know
who'd go to it. Suppose we make up a party and volunteer?
Fourth Businessman I don't mind going if lunch is provided. I must be
fed, if I make one of the party.

The businessmen laugh

First Businessman Well, I'm the most disinterested of you all. I never
  wear black gloves and I never eat lunch. But I'm game for a funeral!
  Come to think of it, I was probably his best friend. (*He laughs*) We used
  to say, "Good morning" to each other occasionally.

A Stock Exchange Clerk hammers on a desk, and shouts out figures.
Another clerk chalks up figures on a board. The Fourth Businessman
looks up at it, through an eye glass

Fourth Businessman Yorkshire Woollens a bit sickly, aren't they?
First Businessman Can't stay gossiping with you fellows. Pleasant as it
  is. Bye, bye...

The businessmen split up

The Spirit points in another direction towards two Important Men who
are talking together

Scrooge follows the Spirit towards them. He moves to listen eagerly to the
Important Men

First Important Man How are you, Staveley?
Second Important Man Pretty well, thank you, Jobbins.
First Important Man Well, I hear the Old Devil has gone to his own at
  last.
Second Important Man I hear, Jobbins. Cold enough for you today, is it?
First Important Man Seasonable for Christmas time, Staveley. You're
  not a skater, I suppose?
Second Important Man No. No, Jobbins. No time for that sort of
  foolishness. I've got some better things to think about. Good morning!
First Important Man Good morning, Staveley!
Scrooge (*to the Spirit*) Ghost! These conversations seem to lack signifi-
  cance. Whose death are they speaking of? Not of Jacob Marley's,
  because that is past. And your province is in the future! All the same, I
  shall do my best to remember what we hear together. I will do my best
  to learn from it.

The Spirit is silent

Still you do not speak to me. Where am I in this future, Spirit? I beg you tell me...

A man in a black coat is standing in a corner, under a clock. He has his back towards us

(*Excitedly*) That's me! That's where I stand on 'Change most mornings. Under the clock. That's my place, Spirit. That's me. Engaged on my business, as usual.

The man turns to face Scrooge. He is a stranger, whom Scrooge does not recognize. The Spirit is standing beside him. He lifts his arm

( ) **Chorus**   Scrooge, fancies, from the turn of the head, that the Phantom's eyes are looking at him keenly.

( ) **Chorus**   It makes him shudder and feel very cold.

( ) **Chorus**   The Spirit leads him into an obscure part of the town, a place of ill repute, where Scrooge has never penetrated before.

Scene 8

Scrooge and the Spirit are in a dark street, pursuing the poorest of the poor

( ) **Chorus**   The ways are foul and narrow, the shops and houses wretched, the people half naked, drunken, slipshod, ugly.

( ) **Chorus**   Alleys and archways, like too many cesspools, disgorge their offences of smell, dirt and life upon the straggling streets...

( ) **Chorus**   And the whole area reeks with crime, with filth and misery.

( ) **Chorus**   In this infamous resort, there is a low-browed, betting shop where iron, rags, bottles, bones, and greasy offal are brought.

We see the filthy shop and Old Joe smoking his pipe, sitting on a stool

( ) **Chorus**   Sitting among his wares is a grey-haired rascal, nearly seventy years of age.

( ) **Chorus**   He smokes his pipe in all the luxury of calm refinement.

Scrooge and the Spirit come into Old Joe's room

A woman with a heavy bundle slinks in through the squeaking, creaking shop door. It is Scrooge's Charwoman

She is followed by a laundress, Mrs Dilber, similarly laden

Next comes a skinny Undertaker's Man in faded black, carrying a smaller bundle

When they have got in, they look at each other in surprised recognition, as they have all come separately, and laugh. Joe joins in their laughter

Charwoman Here's a chance, Old Joe. If we haven't all three met here without meaning it! The Charwoman, the Laundress, the Undertaker's Man.

Joe You couldn't have met in a better place. Come into the parlour! Ha! Ha! We're all suitable to our calling and were well matched. Come into the parlour! (*He pulls aside the tattered curtain of rags*)

They go in. The Charwoman throws her bundle on the floor, sits on a stool and looks defiantly at Mrs Dilber, who stares nervously. Joe pokes up a brazier with a stair rod

Charwoman What's the odds, Mrs Dilber? What're you afraid of? We all have a right to take care of number one. I'm sure *he* did.

Mrs Dilber That's true indeed. No man more so!

Charwoman Well then, don't stand there staring! Let's get on with the business. We're not going to tell tales on each other, I don't suppose.

Mrs Dilber No indeed!

Undertaker's Man We should hope not!

Charwoman And who's the worse for the loss of a few things like these. Not a dead man, I suppose.

Mrs Dilber (*laughing*) No, indeed.

Charwoman And if the wicked old devil wanted them kept after his death, why wasn't he natural and kind during his lifetime? Then he might have had someone to look after him when he was struck down. Instead of lying gasping out his last there, alone and by himself!

Mrs Dilber That's the truest word ever was spoke.

Undertaker's Man It's a judgement on him!

Charwoman It should've been a heavier one, if I could've laid my hands

on anything else! Open the bundle, old Joe. And let me know the value
of it. Speak out plain!
Undertaker's Man Pray let me go first. I have but little plunder...
Charwoman All right, you old burial buzzard. Show us your wares!

*The Undertaker's Man has his bundle open and hands each item to Joe,
who chalks a sum on the wall*

Undertaker's Man Item, a seal.
Joe Five shillings. That's generous.
Undertaker's Man Item, a pencil case and a pair of sleeve buttons. What
can you stretch to?
Joe Half a crown. And not an inch further.
Undertaker's Man Item, a brooch.
Joe Of no great value! Nine pence halfpenny. (*He tots up the figures*)
Eight shilling in all.
Undertaker's Man And threepence halfpenny?
Joe (*counting out money*) And three pence halfpenny, if you insists. And
I wouldn't give another farthing, not if I was to be boiled in oil for it. (*He
gives the Undertaker's Man the money*)

Mrs Dilber opens her bundle

Mrs Dilber There's my items, Joe.
Joe (*looking at them*) Bed sheets. To the number of two. Towels, two.
Underwear apparel, various. (*He puts a finger through a pair of long
johns*) Holier than thou! Silver teaspoons, old fashioned. Sugar tongs,
which don't look as though they had much experience of sugar. Two
pair of boots, in urgent need of the cobbler. Three pound for the lot of
them, and that's stretching it!
Mrs Dilber But...
Joe But that's my weakness. I always stretches for the ladies——

Mrs Dilber seems about to speak

And if you asks me for another penny, I'd repent of being so liberal and
knock off half-a-crown!

He pays Mrs Dilber who takes it with bad grace

Charwoman Now then! You undo *my* bundle, Joe!

Joe kneels to undo the bundle

Joe What you got in here … crown jewels, ain't it? (*He pulls out a heavy roll of dark material*)
Charwoman Articles of great value, old Joe. As you will see when you spreads them out.

Joe holds up the heavy material

Joe What do you call this? Bed curtains?
Charwoman (*laughing, leaning forward on her crossed arm*) Ah! You hit it first time, old Joe. Bed curtains it is.
Joe You don't mean to say you took 'em down, rings and all, with him lying there!
Charwoman Yes, I do. When else could I have done the job, then?

Joe brings the small oil lamp over, and inspects the curtains

Lovely quality they are, as you can see for yourself.
Joe You were born to make your fortune, and you'll certainly do it.
Charwoman I wouldn't stop myself from reaching out for what I wants. Not for the sake of such a man as *he was*. Don't you go getting oil all over these blankets now!
Joe His blankets, is they?
Charwoman He isn't likely to take cold where he is, I dare say.
Joe (*pulling a white shirt out of the bundle*) I hope as he didn't die of anything catching, eh?
Charwoman Only from the meanness and I don't know how infectious that is. Ah. You may look through that shirt till your eyes ache and not find a hole or a threadbare place. It's the best he had. And they'd wasted of it if it hadn't been for me.
Joe What do you call "wasting of it"?
Charwoman Someone was fool enough to put it on him to be buried in. But I took it off again. If rough calico ain't good enough for such a purpose it ain't good enough for anything—and it's quite becoming to a corpse. Anyways. He couldn't look uglier than he did in fine linen.

Joe finds an old flannel bag, then looks in it with delight

Joe And this is where he kept his chinks... Golden guineas, is it?

The Charwoman snatches it from him

Charwoman That's not for sale, Joe! You got your pickings, old man. (*She laughs*) This is the end of it, you see! He frightened everyone away from him while he was alive. So we can profit from his death. I take that very kindly, indeed. (*She laughs*)

The Light dims on the room and concentrates on the shuddering Scrooge and the Spirit

Scrooge I see it now, Spirit! I understand it! The case of the unhappy man they have robbed might be anyone. That is the path my life was taking... (*He cries out*) Merciful heaven. What is this?

SCENE 9

Old Joe's shop has gone and the characters in it. Now we see Scrooge's bed, lit with one cold shaft of light. Lying on it is a body, totally covered with a sheet. And the bed has no curtains

The Spirit is pointing remorselessly at the head of the covered figure on the bed

Scrooge You want me to lift the sheet then, Spirit? You want me to lift it and see the face? I know. A twitch of my finger would do it. Easy. Easy to see who lies there, eh! I wish to obey you, Spirit. I swear I long to do it! Forgive and understand me, Spirit. I cannot find the power to lift my finger and do the work.

The Spirit and Scrooge stand motionless, the Spirit pointing and Scrooge helpless

We see the Chorus in the shadows

( ) **Chorus** Oh, cold, cold, rigid, dreadful death, set up your altar here and dress it with such terrors as you have in your command, for this is your dominion!

( ) **Chorus** No voice says these words in Scrooge's ear. And yet he hears
them when he looks upon the bed.
( ) **Chorus** He thinks that, if this man could be raised up now, what
would be his foremost thoughts?
( ) **Chorus** Avarice, hard dealing, gripping cares? They have brought
him to a rich end truly!
( ) **Chorus** He lies in the dark, in an empty house without a man, a
woman, or a child to say that he was kind to this one or that, or to say
that for the meaning of one kind word, "I will be good to him".

Sound of scratching at a door and under the floorboards

( ) **Chorus** A cat is scratching at the door, and there is a sound of rats
beneath the hearth stone.
( ) **Chorus** What do they want in the room of death, and why are they
so restless and disturbed? Scrooge doesn't dare to think.
Scrooge Spirit! This is a fearful place. In leaving it I shall not forget its
lesson. I beg you. Let us go!

The Spirit is still pointing at the head of the figure on the bed

I said I understand what you want. And I'd do it if I could. But I haven't
the power, Spirit. I have not the power.

The Spirit still points

Is there no-one in this town who feels some emotion, some tenderness,
in the face of death? Show me one person who feels something because
of it! I do beg you, Spirit. Show me!

The Spirit lifts both arms so that its dark robe covers the figure on the bed

SCENE 10

The Cratchits' kitchen

*Mrs Cratchit is doing some embroidery with Martha. Belinda and the
small Cratchits are with them, listening to Peter reading. Scrooge and the
Spirit are watching*

Peter "And he called a little child unto him, and set him in the midst of them. And said, verily, 'I say unto you. Except ye be converted and become as little children, ye shall not enter the kingdom of heaven...'" (*He stops reading*)

Scrooge Where've I heard these words before... I haven't dreamt them! Go on reading...

But Peter closes the book. Mrs Cratchit puts down her work and rubs her eyes

Mrs Cratchit The colour hurts my eyes! They get weak by candlelight.

Belinda Rest a little, Mother.

Mrs Cratchit No. They're better now. (*She picks up her work again*) I wouldn't show weakness to your father when he comes home. It must be near his time.

Peter Rather past it. But he's got a little slower, I think.

Pause

Mrs Cratchit I've known him walk fast with Tiny Tim on his shoulder. Very fast indeed!

Martha Why so have I!

Belinda Often.

Peter So have I.

First Small Cratchit And I.

Second Small Cratchit And me too.

Mrs Cratchit But Tim was very light to carry. And your father loved him. So it was no trouble. No trouble at all.

Sound of the door

That's Father at the door!

Bob Cratchit comes in. He smiles at them all, picks up Mrs Cratchit's work and looks at it

Bob Cratchit So quick with your work, Mother? You'll have it all done by Sunday, you and Martha. (*He sits*)

Martha Sunday!

Mrs Cratchit You went today, then, Robert?

Bob Cratchit Yes, my dear. And I wish you could've been there. It'd've done you good to see how green a place it is. But you'll see it often. I promised him that I would always walk there of a Sunday. (*His voice breaks*) My little, little child. (*He gets up and goes through a door. He enters a bright room hung with Christmas decorations. There is a small bed. We cannot see who is in it*) Tim. (*He stops, and kisses the small face of a little body in a cot. He goes back, through the door to his family, bright and cheerful now*) You'll never guess who I met today!

Cries of "No", "Tell us, Father", "Go on then, Robert", "Who did you meet?", etc.

Mr Scrooge's nephew. And you'll never guess the kindness. He said I seemed a little down. Just a little down, you know. So I had to tell him, about our Tim. And he said—he's just the pleasantest spoken gentleman you ever heard—he said, "I'm heartily sorry for it, Mr Cratchit". And he said "I'm heartily sorry for your good wife". By the way, I can't think how he knew that.

Mrs Cratchit Knew what, my dear.

Bob Cratchit Why, that you're a good wife.

Peter Everyone knows that!

Bob Cratchit Very well observed, my boy. I hope they do. "Heartily sorry," he said, "for your good wife. If I can be of any service," he said. And then he hands me his card, very handsome, I'm sure, all printed and embossed. "That's where I live," he says. "Pray come to me". It wasn't so much for anything he might do, but the kind way he says it which was quite delightful. It was really as if he'd known our Tiny Tim and felt one with us.

Mrs Cratchit I'm sure he's a good man.

Bob Cratchit You would be sure of it, my dear, if ever you was to meet him. I shouldn't be at all surprised, now listen to this, not at all surprised if he didn't get Peter a better situation.

Mrs Cratchit Only hear that, Peter?

Belinda And soon our Peter will be courting and setting up for himself.

Peter (*grinning*) Get along with you, Belinda.

Bob Cratchit It's as likely as not. One of those days. Though there's plenty of time for that, my dear.

Mrs Cratchit One of those days, perhaps.

Bob Cratchit But however we part from one another—I'm sure we won't forget... Not one of us is going to forget ... poor Tiny Tim, shall we?

Cries of "Never, Father", "I'm sure I won't", "Course not", "Never at all", etc.

Nor this first parting among us all.

Cries of "Never, Father", "Never", etc.

Then I'm very happy. Very, very happy.

The family crowd round Bob Cratchit and kiss him. Peter shakes him solemnly by the hand. Light fades on the Cratchit house

SCENE 11

The Lights are up on Scrooge and the Spirit only

Scrooge Spectre. Inform me that our parting moment is at hand. Tell me now. Tell me, Spirit... I beg you. Who was that man we saw lying on the bed?

The Spirit beckons. Scrooge follows

Lights up on the scene we saw at the beginning. The street and Scrooge's front door

Stop a moment! This is where I live. Stop and let me see what shall become of me—in the days to come!

The Spirit moves on, pointing in another direction

That's my house. Why do you point away? That's my office. (*He follows the Spirit*)

Now we can see his office. Scrooge looks in. The furniture has changed and someone else—the man who was standing at Scrooge's corner on the Exchange—is sitting in his chair

I'm not there, Spirit! It's no longer me at work. Earning my daily bread. Where am I? Tell me that quickly!

The Spirit moves on, pointing. Scrooge and the Spirit arrive in a church-yard

The Chorus appear, standing among gravestones, in the shadows

( ) **Chorus** Here, then, the wretched man whose name Scrooge has still to learn, lies underground.
( ) **Chorus** It is a worthy place.
( ) **Chorus** Walled in by houses——
( ) **Chorus** —overrun by grass and weeds...
( ) **Chorus** Choked up by too much burying.
( ) **Chorus** Fat with repleted appetite.
( ) **Chorus** A worthy place.

The Spirit goes to a grave and points down it. Scrooge approaches it, full of fear

Scrooge Spirit... Before I look at that tombstone—answer me one question. Was I the man in the bed? Speak to me, I beg you. Tell me! Are these things the shadows of what *shall* be? Or are they shadows of things that *may* be only?

The Spirit is silent, pointing down to the grave

My behaviour might have led to a certain end. But if I change? If I change myself *completely*...? Then might... Might my end be different? Might it not? I beg you Spirit. Give me a little hope!

The Spirit still points to the neglected grave. Scrooge moves fearfully towards it. And looks. The tombstone is lit brightly. It is very big, made of marble. On it is written "Ebenezer Scrooge R.I.P." Scrooge falls on his knees

Am I the man who lay on the bed? Am I? Tell me the worst of it, Spirit.

The Spirit points to Scrooge, then to the tombstone, and back again to Scrooge

No, Spirit. Oh no, no! Not I! (*He clutches the Spirit's robe*) Spirit. I'm
not the man I was! I'm someone else now. Someone else entirely. I
won't be the man I might have been, if I'd never had the pleasure of
meeting you, Sprit. Why do you show me this—if I'm past all hope and
lost forever?

For the first time, the Spirit's hand shakes a little uncertainly

Good Spirit! Your kind nature pities me. You'll intercede for me. Tell
me I can change these shadows you've shown to me. Tell me I can still
change!

The Spirit's hand trembles a little

I promise you! My solemn oath! I'll honour Christmas and try to keep
it all the year. I will live truly in the past, the present and the future. The
spirits of all three shall strive within me! I shall not shut out the lesson
they teach me. Oh Spirit. Kind Spirit! Tell me I may sponge away the
writing on that stone! (*He catches the Spirit's hand*)

*The Light begins to fade. The Spirit tries to free itself, and succeeds at last.
Scrooge holds up his hands in prayer—and the Spirit starts to collapse,
grow small and become—Scrooge's bedpost*

SCENE 12

Scrooge's bedroom is flooded with Light

*Scrooge is feeling his bedpost, looking at his bed and his room with
increasing and ecstatic delight*

Scrooge Yes! Oh yes... The bed's your own, Ebenezer, old fellow. The
room's your own! And you know what? *Do* you know what, you old
skin-flint as was? The time before you is your own! To make amends
in... (*He sees the bed curtains, still on the bed and embraces them*) Not
torn down! Never torn down and sold. They're still with me, rings and
all! My bed curtains are here! Ebenezer Scrooge is here. The shadows
of what might have been will vanish away—I know they will! (*His voice
breaks, he's almost sobbing*) From now on... From this day on, I'll live

in the Past, the Present and the Future! The Spirits of all of them shall strive within me! (*He falls to his knees*) Oh, Jacob Marley, Heaven and Christmas Time be praised for this! (*He lifts his hands in prayer*) I say it on my knees, old Jacob! On my knees. (*He struggles to his feet and starts to dress*) I don't know what to do! (*He is laughing and crying, scattering his clothes*) I am as light as a feather. I am as happy as an angel. I am as larky as a schoolboy! (*He finds his long johns, puts his finger through the hole in them, throws them into a corner and gets out a new pair. All this time he's getting dressed under his night-gown, like a modest bather, and getting extremely tied up in the process*) I'm as giddy ... as a drunken man. As jolly as a Jack Tar. Merry as a gig... Happy as a man weeding the asparagus. Jolly as a jumping bean... Laughing like a drain. Dancing like a dervish. A Merry Christmas all round! A Happy New Year to all the world! (*He looks round him again*) It's all here! Look at it. All here... The saucepan for my little bit of gruel. Old Jacob Marley came through *here*. And the Ghost of Christmas Present sat in *there*... (*He scratches his head*) I don't know what day of the month it is. I don't know how long I've been among the spirits. Don't know anything. I'm quite a baby. Never mind. Don't care. Best thing to be, no doubt, a baby! Quite the best! (*He goes to the window*) And here's the window where I saw the wandering spirits. It's all true! It all happened. Ha! Ha! Ha! (*He opens the window*)

There is a loud peal of church bells. We see the street, lit with bright winter sunshine

No more fog! No mist! Clear. Bright. Jovial. Stirring. Cold. Cold. Piping for the blood to dance to. Golden sunlight. Heavenly sky. Sweet fresh air. Merry bells. Oh, glorious! Glorious!

People fill the street

A Boy in Sunday clothes loiters under Scrooge's window

(*Calling to the Boy*) Whoop! Hallo. Here! What's today?
Boy Eh?
Scrooge What's today, my fine fellow, my lad?
Boy Today? Why, it's Christmas Day.
Scrooge (*turning away from the window; to himself*) It's Christmas Day! I haven't missed it! The Spirits have done all their work in one night. Of

course. They can do anything they like, of course they can! (*He puts his head out of the window*) Hallo again, my fine fellow!

Boy (*a little wearily*) Hallo.

Scrooge Do you know the Poulterers in the next street but one?

Boy I should hope I did.

Scrooge An intelligent boy! A remarkable boy! A boy of enormous brain! A boy to breed from! Do you happen to know, hopeful sir, whether they've sold the Prize Turkey that was hanging up there? Not the little Prize Turkey. I mean the big Prize Turkey!

Boy What, the one as big as me?

Scrooge What a delightful boy. It's a pleasure to talk to him! Yes, my buck.

Boy It hangs there at this very moment.

Scrooge Does it indeed! Then nip round and buy it, will you? For Mr Scrooge.

Boy Are you serious?

Scrooge Deadly serious! I do assure you. And, oh, excellent boy! Go and buy it, and tell 'em to bring it here, that I may give them directions where to take it. Come back with the man and I'll give you a shilling!

The Boy hesitates

Come back in less than five minutes and I'll give you half-a-crown.

Boy I'm off like a shot!

The Boy dashes off

Scrooge looks after him. He then finds hot water left by his door, pours it into a bowl and starts to shave, trembling with excitement

Scrooge I'll send it to Bob Cratchit. Cratchit; Two, Scrivener's Passage, Camden Town. I believe that's it. Yes! That's it. He shan't know who sends it. (*He laughs*) Careless! Nearly had my nose off then. Last person he'll think made him such a present is old skin-flint, Scrooge. He'll think a magnificent bird dropped on his family from the sky! Why it's a fowl twice the size of Tiny Tim. Grimaldi in the pantomime never thought up such a joke as my sending a prize turkey anonymous to Bob Cratchit! I hope it bastes well and they serves it up with sausages! (*He wipes the lather off his face and appears smiling at his front door. As he does so he notices the door knocker*) Dear old door knocker! I scarcely

ever looked at you before but I'll love you as long as I live. What an
honest expression you had on your face last night! And how handsome
old Jacob was to be sure! And how you can change your appearance—
you wonderful knocker. Hallo!

*The Boy appears, followed by the Poulterer's Man, bent almost double
under the weight of a huge turkey*

Scrooge looks at it and pinches it with glee

Now that is a turkey! That bird could never have stood on his legs!
He'd've snapped them off in a minute like sticks of sealing wax.
Poulterer's Man Where is it to go to, sir?
Scrooge Scrivener's Passage. Camden Town. Name of Cratchit. And
never breathe a word as to who sent it.
Poulterer's Man (*almost collapsing*) Never breathe a word ... sir.
Scrooge Why you can't carry that monster to Camden Town! Not even
Hercules could do it. You must have a cab. Likeable and efficient, Boy,
will you call me a cab?

The Boy hesitates again

Boy You're a cab, sir!
Scrooge Delightful boy! Here's money for the cab. And for the bird. And
half a crown for the Young Sparkler here, as promised. (*He hands out
money to the Boy and the Poulterer's Man*)

The Boy runs off, his fingers in his mouth, emitting a piercing whistle

The Poulterer's Man staggers unsteadily under the bird

Scrooge walks among the crowd with his hands behind his back, smiling

*The Chorus, who are all out on the street now, nod and smile back and
speak in turn*

( ) **Chorus** The people are pouring forth...
( ) **Chorus** As he had seen them with the Ghost of Christmas Present.
( ) **Chorus** And Scrooge walks among them with his hands behind his
back, greeting everyone with a delighted smile.

( ) **Chorus** He looks so irresistibly pleasant, that three or four people say...

( ) **Chorus** (*to Scrooge*) Good morning, sir!

( ) **Chorus** (*to Scrooge*) Good morning, sir. And a Merry Christmas!

Scrooge (*stopping; thoughtfully*) Of all the blithe sounds I ever heard, those words were the blithest to my ears.

The two Portly Gentlemen are walking in his direction

Scrooge looks nervously at them

( ) **Chorus** Then he saw the Portly Gentlemen!

Scrooge walks up to the Portly Gentlemen and shakes them both by the hand

Scrooge My dear sirs! It was exceeding kind of you to call on me yesterday. I hope you succeeded well. A Merry Christmas to you. And to you, sir. A Merry Christmas!

First Portly Gent (*incredulously*) Mr Scrooge?

Second Portly Gent *Is* it, Mr Scrooge?

Scrooge Yes, oh yes, indeed. That is my name. And I fear it may not be pleasant to you. Allow me to ask your pardon. And, if you will have patience with me for a moment, may I suggest a modest sum, for which you may put me down—a small contribution? (*He whispers in the First Portly Gentleman's ear*)

First Portly Gent Mr Scrooge... Did you say a *modest* sum?

Scrooge whispers in the Second Portly Gentleman's ear

Second Portly Gent (*amazed*) Mr Scrooge... Did you say a *small* contribution?

First Portly Gent Lord bless us. Mr Scrooge! Are you serious?

Scrooge If you please. Not a farthing less! A great many back payments are included in it, I do assure you. Now then, do me a favour, and say no more about it.

First Portly Gent We don't know what to say to such a munifice——

Scrooge Don't say anything, please. Come and see me.

First Portly Gent We will.

Scrooge Will you come and see me?

Second Portly Gent We will.

Scrooge Thankee. Thankee, gentlemen both. Much obliged to you, I'm
sure. Thankee fifty times. Bless you!

The church bells ring

Scrooge joins the people going into church

SCENE 13

Scrooge's Nephew's drawing-room

*The Nephew is putting up Christmas decorations, the Niece is helping the
Maid lay out wine glasses, etc. We see people, including the Chorus, in the
street outside*

*Scrooge appears in the street, walking and enjoying himself. He pats
children on the head, questions beggars and looks down into the kitchens
of houses, up to the windows and finds that everything could yield him
pleasure*

(   ) **Chorus** He had never dreamed that any walk——
(   ) **Chorus** That *anything*——
(   ) **Chorus** —could give him so much happiness.
(   ) **Chorus** In the afternoon, he turns his steps towards his nephew's
house.

We see Scrooge approach the door. He hesitates about going in

(   ) **Chorus** He passes the door many times before he has the courage to
go up and knock.
(   ) **Chorus** Then he makes a dash and does it!

*Scrooge knocks on the Nephew's door. The Maid comes and opens the
door*

Scrooge Is your master at home, my dear? Nice girl! Very.
Maid Yes, sir.
Scrooge Where is he, my love?

Maid He's in the drawing-room, sir. Along with the mistress. I'll show you the way, if you please.

Scrooge Thankee. He knows me. I'll go in then, my dear. (*He goes in. He opens the drawing-room door a crack, and sidles his face in round the door, then calls out in a deep ghostly voice*) Fred...! Are you there, Fred?

The Niece looks startled and drops a glass. Fred looks round from hanging a decoration

Nephew God bless my soul, who's that?

Scrooge (*still ghostly*) It is I! Your Uncle Scrooge, come to dinner! (*In a normal voice*) Will you let me in, Fred? (*To Niece*) Sorry to surprise you, my dear.

Nephew (*greeting him, pumping his hand*) Let you in! Why welcome, Uncle. A thousand times welcome. My dear, it's Uncle Scrooge. Uncle Scrooge. Come to dinner at last!

Scrooge Wonders will never cease, eh?

Niece (*smiling*) You're very welcome, Uncle Scrooge.

Scrooge Thankee, my dear. I take that very kindly.

Nephew Why don't you give her a kiss for it, Uncle Scrooge...

Scrooge Shall I? I take that kindly, very kindly indeed. (*He kisses his Niece*) Thankee. Expecting a party aren't we? Games and all the jollity?

There's a knock at the door

The guests arrive and are led in by the Maid. Topper and the Niece's sisters, including the plump one with the lace tucker, come in

Scrooge greets them

Ah, Mr Topper! I hope I see you well, sir. Ebenezer Scrooge's my name. Fred's Uncle Scrooge. I had the honour to appear in a game of animal vegetable and mineral which didn't have to happen... And my dear niece's sisters... (*To the plump one*) I have to warn you, my dear, to be particularly watchful of Mr Topper. Well, we all have something to look forward to tonight, eh... Wonderful party! Wonderful unanimity. Wonderful jollity!

Nephew I think we can promise you that, Uncle...

Scrooge And wonderful games! Do you think we could have one now? Just a small one to kick off the proceedings?

The guests all laugh. The Nephew pulls out a handkerchief and blindfolds Scrooge, and spins him round. Scrooge is laughing, trying to catch the Niece's sisters as they laugh and skip out of his way

The Light fades on the Nephew's drawing-room

( ) **Chorus** Wonderful happiness!
( ) **Chorus** They all go late to bed.
( ) **Chorus** Tired out by the joy of the occasion.
( ) **Chorus** But Scrooge is early at his office next morning.

SCENE 14

Scrooge is approaching his office, walking fast, looking at his watch

( ) **Chorus** Oh, he's early now.
( ) **Chorus** If only he can be first in and catch Bob Cratchit coming late!
( ) **Chorus** That's what he's set his heart on.
( ) **Chorus** And he does it!

The clock strikes and Scrooge goes into his office

( ) **Chorus** Just as the clock is striking nine.

Scrooge sits at his desk. He looks severe and business-like. He starts to work

( ) **Chorus** Nine o'clock and no Bob Cratchit!

The clock strikes a quarter

( ) **Chorus** Quarter past and still no Bob!
( ) **Chorus** Scrooge sits with his door open so he might see his clerk come into the tank.

Scrooge looks at his watch

*Bob Cratchit comes running towards the office. He has his hat off and
his muffler off as he runs into his little tank-like office*

Scrooge Hallo... Cratchit! What do you mean by coming in at this time
of day?

Bob Cratchit I'm very sorry, sir. I *am* behind my time.

Scrooge (*looking at his watch*) Are you? Yes, I think you are. A full
eighteen and a half minutes behind your time.

Bob comes into Scrooge's office, deeply apologetic and fearful

Bob Cratchit It's only once a year, sir. It shall not be repeated. I was
making rather merry yesterday, if you please, sir.

Scrooge Now I'll tell you what, my friend! I'm not going to stand for this
sort of thing any longer... And therefore...

*Scrooge jumps off his stool and gives Bob such a dig in the ribs that he
staggers back towards the tank*

And therefore I am going to raise your salary!

Bob puts out his hand and feels for Scrooge's ruler

( ) **Chorus** Now Bob has no doubt that his master has taken complete
leave of his senses.

( ) **Chorus** He has a momentary idea of knocking Scrooge down with his
own ruler.

( ) **Chorus** And calling out to the people in the Court for help and a strait-
jacket.

Scrooge (*shaking Bob's hand and clasping him on the shoulder*) A Merry
Christmas, Bob... A merrier Christmas, Bob, my good fellow, than I
have given you for many years...

Bob Cratchit Are you sure you're feeling quite ... yourself, Mr Scrooge?

Scrooge My new self, Bob! My old self no longer. I'll raise your salary!
And I'll try and help your struggling family! We'll talk about that this
afternoon, over a Christmas bowl of mulled wine, good and spicy. But
before all this, Bob, in the name of sanity, make up the fire and buy
another coal scuttle before you dot another "i" or cross another "t". Bob
Cratchit.

Bob Cratchit looks at him, and then starts to laugh. Scrooge laughs with him. Light fades on Scrooge's office

SCENE 15

( ) **Chorus** At the end of it, old Scrooge is better than his word.

( ) **Chorus** He does it all, and infinitely more.

( ) **Chorus** He becomes as good a friend, as good a master, and as good a man, as the good old city knows.

( ) **Chorus** Or any other good old city, town, or borough, in the good old world...

Light, sunshine, snow

The Chorus queue up to slide on the ice

The whole Cratchit family are there, by a brazier, roasting chestnuts. Mrs Cratchit has a basket of bottles and buns. Tiny Tim is there, the Portly Gentlemen, the Nephew and Niece and other characters. Scrooge is standing at the end of the slide

The Chorus say their lines as they come on to the slide and then slide towards Scrooge

( ) **Chorus** Some people laughed to see the alteration in him, but he lets them laugh and little eeds them!

( ) **Chorus** For he is wise enough to know that nothing good ever happened on this globe, at which some people did not have their fill of laughter.

( ) **Chorus** His own heart laughs and that's quite enough for him.

Bob Cratchit Now Scrooge is a second father to Tiny Tim. Who did *not* die!

The Chorus starts to sing a carol. Bob Cratchit takes Tim's crutch. Scrooge holds his hands and helps him slide down the ice. Mrs Cratchit is busy handing out drinks and buns

Mrs Cratchit A taste of rum for you, Mr Scrooge? Just to keep out the cold.

Scrooge Thankee. I've decided to give up the Spirits forever.

The three Spirits appear above the slide

Everyone joins in the carol

Spirit Of Christmas Present It's always said of Scrooge that he knows to keep Christmas well, if any man alive possesses the knowledge. May that be truly said of us, and all of us.
Tiny Tim God bless us, *everyone*!

The Carol swells. Everyone is singing

CURTAIN

FURNITURE AND PROPERTY LIST

ACT I

SCENE 1

On stage: Coffin
Soil
Sign: "Scrooge and Marley"

Personal: **Prosperous Man:** money

SCENE 2

Strike: Coffin
Soil
Sign: "Scrooge and Marley"

Set: **Scrooge**'s desk with lockable drawer. *On it:* huge ledger, ruler
Large tin box with lock and key. *In it:* money
Burning candle
Cratchit's table
Shovel
Matches
Cratchit's scarf and hat
Scrooge's hat and coat

Personal: **Scrooge:** pen
Portly Gentlemen: hats
First Portly Gentleman: paper

SCENE 3

Strike: **Scrooge**'s desk with lockable drawer. *On it:* huge ledger, ruler
Large tin box with lock and key. *In it:* money
Burning candle
Cratchit's table

Shovel
Matches

Set: Brazier
            Chophouse furniture

Off stage: Chop, newspaper (**Waiter**)
            Bank book (**Scrooge**)
            Toothpick (**Waiter**)

Personal: **Tiny Tim:** crutch
            Scrooge: money

SCENE 4

Strike: Brazier
            Chophouse furniture

Set: Candle

Personal: **Scrooge:** key
            Marley: spectacles

SCENE 5

Set: Curtained bed
            Slippers
            Chair
            Night clothes
            Fireplace
            Bowl of gruel
            Bell

Personal: **Marley's Ghost:** chain with keys, padlocks, ledgers, deeds and
            heavy purses

SCENE 6

On stage: As before

Personal: **The Ghost:** safe

SCENE 7

Set: Watch

Off stage: Giant dunce's cap, large candle snuffer (**Spirit of Christmas Past**)

SCENE 8

Strike: Curtained bed
                Chair
                Fireplace
                Bowl of gruel
                Bell
                Watch

SCENE 9

Set: Cupboard
                Coach

Off stage: Book (**Child Scrooge**)
                Trunk (**Servant**)
                Glasses, sherry (**Headmaster**)

Personal: **Robinson Crusoe:** gun, parrot

SCENE 10

Strike: Cupboard
                Coach
                Book
                Trunk
                Glasses
                Sherry

Set: Counter
                Cupboards. *In them:* beds
                Tall desk
                Chair
                Sacks
                Packing cases

Off stage: Table. *On it:* food, drink (**Cook**)

Personal: **Mr Fezziwig:** money, sweets
                 Fiddler: fiddle

Scene 11

Strike: Counter
                 Cupboards. *In them:* beds
                 Tall desk
                 Chair
                 Sacks
                 Packing cases
                 Table. *On it:* food, drink

Set: 2 couches

Off stage: Parcels (**Belle's Husband**)

Scene 12

Set: Curtained bed

ACT II

Scene 1

Strike: 2 couches

Set: Throne
                 Holly
                 Mistletoe
                 Piles of chickens, turkeys, fruit
                 Steaming bowl of punch

Personal: **Spirit:** torch

Scene 2

Strike: Throne
                 Holly
                 Mistletoe

90 A Christmas Carol

Piles of chickens, turkeys, fruit
Steaming bowl of punch

Set: Spades
Piles of fruit and food

Off stage: Dinners under covers: steaming birds, joints (**Shoppers**)
Dinner under a cover: very small goose (**Small Cratchits**)

Personal: **Spirit:** torch

SCENE 3

Strike: Spades
Piles of fruit and food

Set: Fire
Broom cupboard
Table
Pot of potatoes
Crockery
Cutlery
Steaming bowl of punch
Glasses

Off stage: **Tiny Tim's** crutch (**Bob Cratchit**)
Dinner under a cover: very small goose (**Small Cratchits**)
Small flaming pudding (**Mrs Cratchit**)

Personal: **Spirit:** torch

SCENE 4

Strike: Fire
Broom cupboard
Pot of potatoes
Crockery
Cutlery
Steaming bowl of punch
Glasses
Tiny Tim's crutch

Dinner under a cover: very small goose
Small flaming pudding

SCENE 5

Set: Big fire
              Drinks
              Ladle
              Roasting chestnuts and other party foods

Personal: **Scrooge's Nephew:** handkerchief
              Scrooge: handkerchief

SCENE 6

Strike: Big fire
              Drinks
              Ladle
              Roasting chestnuts and other party foods

SCENE 7

On stage: Boards with share prices
              Desk
              Clock

Off stage: Lists (**Businessmen**)

Personal: **Stock Exchange Clerk:** chalk
              Fourth Businessman: eye glass

SCENE 8

Strike: Boards with share prices
              Desk
              Clock

Set: Stools
              Brazier

              Stair rod
              Small oil lamp

Off stage: Heavy bundle. *In it:* bed curtains, white shirt, old flannel bag
              (Charwoman)
              Heavy bundle. *In it:* bed sheets, underwear, silver teaspoons, sugar
              tongs, two pairs of boots **(Mrs Dilber)**
              Smaller bundle. *In it:* seal, pencil case, pair of sleeve buttons, brooch
              (Undertaker's Man)

Personal: **Old Joe:** pipe, money

SCENE 9

Strike: Stools
              Brazier
              Stair rod
              Small oil lamp
              Heavy bundle. *In it:* bed curtains, white shirt, old flannel bag
              Heavy bundle. *In it:* bed sheets, underwear, silver teaspoons, sugar
              tongs, two pairs of boots
              Smaller bundle. *In it:* seal, pencil case, pair of sleeve buttons, brooch

Set: **Scrooge**'s bed

SCENE 10

Strike: **Scrooge**'s bed without curtains

Set: Fire
              Broom cupboard
              Table
              Crockery
              Cutlery
              Embroidery
              Book
              Christmas decorations
              Small bed

SCENE 11

Strike: Fire
                Broom cupboard
                Table
                Crockery
                Cutlery
                Embroidery
                Book
                Christmas decorations
                Small bed

Set: Office furniture
                Gravestones
                Large gravestone with inscription "Ebenezer Scrooge R.I.P."

SCENE 12

Strike: Office furniture
                Gravestones
                Large gravestone with inscription "Ebenezer Scrooge R.I.P."

Set: **Scrooge**'s bed
                Clothes
                Slippers
                Chair
                Fireplace
                Bowl of gruel
                Bell
                Hot water in a container
                Bowl
                Razor
                Lather
                Towel

Off stage: Huge turkey (**Poulterer's Man**)

Personal: **Scrooge:** money

SCENE 13

Strike:	**Scrooge**'s bed
	Clothes
	Slippers
	Chair
	Fireplace
	Bowl of gruel
	Bell
	Hot water in a container
	Bowl
	Razor
	Lather
	Towel
	Huge turkey
Set:	Christmas decorations
	Wine glasses
Personal:	**Scrooge's Nephew:** handkerchief

SCENE 14

Strike:	Christmas decorations
	Wine glasses
Set:	Desk. *On it:* ledger, pen, ruler
	Stool

SCENE 15

Strike:	Desk. *On it:* ledger, pen, ruler
	Stool
Set:	Brazier. *On it:* roasting chestnuts
	Basket. *In it:* bottles, buns
Off stage:	Prop (**Character**)
Personal:	**Tiny Tim:** crutch

LIGHTING PLOT

Property fittings required: fire in Scrooge's sitting room; cooking fire in Cratchits' kitchen; fire in Nephew's living-room, brazier, small oil-lamp Various interior and exterior settings

ACT I

To open: Overall general lighting

Cue 1	**Chorus**: "...Or the coffin nail, perhaps." *Cross-fade to* **Scrooge**'s *office*	(Page 3)
Cue 2	**Chorus**: "...take advantage over him." *Bring up lights on Bob Cratchit's small office*	(Page 4)
Cue 3	**Scrooge** rules lines on paper *Bleaker light outside*	(Page 9)
Cue 4	**Singers**: "O tidings of comfort and joy." *Cross-fade to street; evening lighting*	(Page 11)
Cue 5	**Chorus**: "Not a knocker, but..." *Projection of* **Marley**'s *face on door knocker*	(Page 14)
Cue 6	**Scrooge**: "You're dead as a coffin nail, remember." *Fade out projection*	(Page 14)
Cue 7	**Scrooge** stops *Projection of a hearse on a wall*	(Page 15)
Cue 8	**Scrooge** moves up to his bedroom *Cross-fade to* **Scrooge**'s *bedroom and sitting-room; low fire effect*	(Page 15)
Cue 9	**Chorus**: "...were drawn aside..." *Bring up strange light from the top of the* **Spirit of Christmas Past**'s *head*	(Page 21)

Cue 10   **Scrooge** and **The Spirit** walk round the stage   (Page 23)
            Bring up clear winter sunshine

Cue 11   **Scrooge**: "I know him!"   (Page 24)
            Bring up school lighting; in the country

Cue 12   The country turns into a city   (Page 28)
            Bring up city lighting

Cue 13   **Dick Wilkins** and **Young Scrooge** shut cupboard doors   (Page 35)
            Fade out lights

Cue 14   **Chorus**: "...growing tree would fall."   (Page 35)
            Bring up drawing-room lighting

Cue 15   **Young Scrooge** stands alone   (Page 37)
            Fade lights down

Cue 16   **Scrooge**: "Show me no more."   (Page 37)
            Lights up on a couch

Cue 17   **Belle's Husband**: "...alone in the world, I do believe." (Page 38)
            Fade out drawing-room lights

Cue 18   **Scrooge** pulls the curtains shut   (Page 39)
            Black-out

ACT II

To open: Lighting on **Scrooge**'s bedroom

Cue 19   **Chorus**: "...and no shape appears..."   (Page 40)
            Bring up red light on **Scrooge**'s *bed*

Cue 20   **Scrooge** opens a door into a room at the foot of the stairs (Page 41)
            Snap on red light in the room, as though lit by a huge fire

Cue 21   **Scrooge** and **The Spirit** rise in the air   (Page 42)
            Fade out red lights

Cue 22   **Scrooge** and **The Spirit** are gone   (Page 45)
            Cross-fade to the Cratchits' kitchen; cooking fire effect

Cue 23   **Tiny Tim**: "God bless us everyone."   (Page 48)
             Fade out lights, then bring up when ready

Cue 24   **Tiny Tim** stands and sings *If Bethlehem*   (Page 50)
             Slowly fade general lights; sprinkle **The Spirit**'s
             light on **Tiny Tim**

Cue 25   **Spirit**: "...and contented with the time..."   (Page 50)
             Slowly fade out lights, with the light on **Tiny Tim** *going
             out last*

Cue 26   The **Chorus** come on   (Page 50)
             Bring up general lighting

Cue 27   **Company** (*singing*): "On Christmas Day in the morning."   (Page 52)
             Lighthouse beam moves across the sky

Cue 28   **Chorus**: "...like the waves they skim."   (Page 52)
             Bring up fire lighting on the **Lighthouse Men**

Cue 29   **Scrooge** and **The Spirit** move on   (Page 53)
             Cross-fade to a scene at sea

Cue 30   **Chorus**: "...with approving affability!"   (Page 54)
             Cross-fade to **Nephew**'s *living room; fire effect*

Cue 31   **Scrooge** and **The Spirit** go   (Page 60)
             Fade out lights

Cue 32   **Chorus**: "That night Scrooge and the Spirit travel far."   (Page 60)
             Bring up background lighting; projection of distant city

Cue 33   **Chorus**: "...Scrooge has never penetrated before."   (Page 65)
             Cross-fade to dark street lighting

Cue 34   **Chorus**: "...and greasy offal are brought."   (Page 65)
             Bring up lighting on **Old Joe**'s *shop; brazier effect*

Cue 35   **Charwoman** laughs   (Page 69)
             Fade out dark street and shop lighting; spot on
             Scrooge *and* **The Spirit**

Cue 36   **Old Joe**'s shop and the characters in it are gone   (Page 69)
             Cross-fade to one cold shaft of light on **Scrooge**'s *bed*

Cue 37   **The Spirit** lifts both arms   (Page 70)
            Cross-fade to **Cratchits'** *kitchen*

Cue 38   **Bob Cratchit** goes through a door   (Page 72)
            Snap on bright light in the room

Cue 39   **Peter** shakes **Bob Cratchit's** hand   (Page 73)
            Cross-fade to lights on **Scrooge** *and* **The Spirit** *only*

Cue 40   **Scrooge** follows **The Spirit**   (Page 73)
            Lights up on the street

Cue 41   **Scrooge** looks at the neglected grave   (Page 74)
            Spotlight on tombstone

Cue 42   **Scrooge** catches **The Spirit's** hand   (Page 75)
            Slowly fade out lights

Cue 43   **The Spirit** becomes **Scrooge's** bedpost   (Page 75)
            Bring up bright lights on **Scrooge's** *bedroom*

Cue 44   **Scrooge** opens the window   (Page 76)
            Bright winter sunshine outside

Cue 45   **Scrooge** joins the people going into church   (Page 80)
            Cross-fade to **The Nephew's** *drawing-room*

Cue 46   **Scrooge** tries to catch the Niece's sisters   (Page 82)
            Fade light on **The Nephew's** *drawing-room*

Cue 47   **Chorus**: "…early at his office next morning."   (Page 82)
            Bring up street and **Scrooge's** *office lighting*

Cue 48   **Scrooge** laughs   (Page 84)
            Fade lights on **Scrooge's** *office*

Cue 49   **Chorus**: "…in the good old werld…"   (Page 84)
            Bring up sunlight effect; brazier effect

EFFECTS PLOT

ACT I

Cue 1   To open Scene 1   (Page 3)
        Fog rises outside and lock strikes three

Cue 2   **Scrooge** rules lines on paper   (Page 9)
        Snow effect

Cue 3   **Scrooge** goes back to work   (Page 10)
        Clock strikes six

Cue 4   **Chorus**: "…people run about with flaring links."   (Page 11)
        Fog effect

Cue 5   **The Waiter** makes rude gestures   (Page 12)
        Music: "Alas We Bless"

Cue 6   **Scrooge** slams the door shut   (Page 14)
        Echoes of "Pooh! Pooh!" and the sound of the door

Cue 7   **Chorus**: "But now it rings out loudly!"   (Page 16)
        *Bell in **Scrooge**'s sitting-room rings, then every bell
           in the house rings*

Cue 8   **Scrooge**: "I won't believe it."   (Page 16)
        Bells stop ringing; sound of a door slamming

Cue 9   **Chorus**: "Who slams the door?"   (Page 16)
        Sound of chains being dragged across the floor

Cue 10   **Marley**'s **Ghost** goes up the stairs   (Page 16)
        Sound of his footsteps

Cue 11   **Marley**'s **Ghost** rattles his chain   (Page 17)
        Amplify sound of the chain

Cue 12   **Marley**'s **Ghost**'s jaw drops on to its chest   (Page 17)
        Clang

Cue 13   **Scrooge**: "It's getting late and I've been hard at work."   (Page 17)
            Unearthly music

Cue 14   **Scrooge**: "You was always a good businessman."   (Page 18)
            Cut music

Cue 15   **Marley**'s **Ghost**'s teeth snap together   (Page 19)
            Loud effect

Cue 16   The window opens of its own accord 1   (Page 19)
            *Sound of wailing and lamentation
               (may be performed live)*

Cue 17   **Scrooge** shuts the bed curtains   (Page 20)
            Church clock chimes a quarter; music: "Veni, Veni"

Cue 18   **Scrooge** peers out of the bed   (Page 20)
            Clock chimes second quarter

Cue 19   **Scrooge**: "When I got there..."   (Page 20)
            Clock chimes three-quarters

Cue 20   **Scrooge**: "Dark as hell at Christmas."   (Page 20)
            Clock chimes the hour

Cue 21   **Scrooge**: "And nothing else."   (Page 21)
            One deep, hollow clock boom

Cue 22   **Scrooge** and **The Spirit** rise into the air   (Page 23)
            Mist effect, clear when ready

Cue 23   **Scrooge** disappears again among the dancers   (Page 33)
            Clock strikes eleven

Cue 24   **Belle**: "...I don't mind it at all."   (Page 37)
            Sound of a door

ACT II

Cue 25   **Chorus**: "...prepared for nothing!"   (Page 40)
            Clock strikes one

Cue 26   **Spirit**: "Touch my robe."   (Page 42)
            Music: "All Hail to the Days"

Cue 27   **Chorus**: "...in the best humour possible."   (Page 43)
          Church bells, then a sound of a distant organ

Cue 28   **Peter** blows up the fire under the potatoes   (Page 45)
          Shower of sparks

Cue 29   **Spirit**: "Tonight at midnight."   (Page 60)
          Clock chimes three-quarters

Cue 30   **Spirit**: "Do you remember who said that, Scrooge?"   (Page 62)
          Clock strikes twelve and mist rises

Cue 31   **Scrooge** and **The Spirit** move towards the City   (Page 63)
          Stock Exchange clamour and voices
          (may be performed live)

Cue 32   **Chorus**: "I will be good to him."   (Page 70)
          Scratching at a door and under the floorboards

Cue 33   **Mrs Cratchit**: "No trouble at all."   (Page 71)
          Sound of the door

Cue 34   **Scrooge** opens the window   (Page 76)
          Loud peal of church bells

Cue 35   **Scrooge**: "Bless you!"   (Page 80)
          Church bells ring

Cue 36   **Chorus**: "And he does it!"   (Page 82)
          Clock strikes

Cue 37   **Chorus**: "Nine o'clock and no Bob Cratchit!"   (Page 82)
          Clock strikes a quarter

Cue 38   **Chorus**: "...in the good old world..."   (Page 84)
          Snow effect

MADE AND PRINTED IN GREAT BRITAIN BY
LATIMER TREND & COMPANY LTD PLYMOUTH

MADE IN ENGLAND